# A DELICIOUS TEMPTATION

Kissing wasn't new for Mery. She'd been stealing kisses since she was twelve. So her first instinct wasn't necessarily to fight him.

It wasn't her second instinct either.

And the longer the kiss went on, the less she thought about fighting him at all.

This work is a work of fiction. Names, places, characters and incidents are the product of the author's imagination or are used fictitiously. Any resemblance to actual events, locales or persons, living or dead, is coincidental.

MacKENZIE'S LASS



Glynnis Campbell – Publisher
P.O. Box 341144
Arleta, California 91331
Contact: glynnis@glynnis.net

Cover design by Richard Campbell
Formatting by Author E.M.S.

ISBN-13: 978-1-63480-086-0

Published in the United States of America

# MACKENZIE'S LASS

The Scottish Lasses, Book 3

GLYNNIS CAMPBELL

# DEDICATION

*For Sandy Easson
And all the rest of the lovely folks
I've met in Scotland
Who've opened their arms and hearts*

# OTHER BOOKS BY GLYNNIS CAMPBELL

**THE WARRIOR MAIDS OF RIVENLOCH**
The Shipwreck (novella)
A Yuletide Kiss (short story)
Lady Danger
Captive Heart
Knight's Prize

**THE WARRIOR DAUGHTERS OF RIVENLOCH**
The Storming (novella)
A Rivenloch Christmas (short story)
Bride of Fire
Bride of Ice
Bride of Mist

**THE WARRIOR LAIRDS OF RIVENLOCH**
Laird of Steel
Laird of Flint
Laird of Smoke

**THE KNIGHTS OF DE WARE**
The Handfasting (novella)
My Champion
My Warrior
My Hero

**MEDIEVAL OUTLAWS**
The Reiver (novella)
Danger's Kiss
Passion's Exile
Desire's Ransom

**THE SCOTTISH LASSES**
The Outcast (novella)
MacFarland's Lass
MacAdam's Lass
MacKenzie's Lass

**THE CALIFORNIA LEGENDS**
Native Gold
Native Wolf
Native Hawk

# ACKNOWLEDGMENTS

Special thanks to:

Eleanor Muir
Visitor Experience Manager at Stirling Castle

Sandy Easson
Tudor Chef at Stirling Castle

Finlay Lumsden
Manager of Campbell Castle

Nicky Saunders
Madrigal Singer


Christian Kane and Rachel McAdams

# CHAPTER 1

**DECEMBER 16, 1566**
**STIRLING CASTLE, SCOTLAND**

Through the smoky haze of the crowded roasting room, Tristan MacKenzie frowned at the turnbrochie dozing by the fire.

Turning the spit for hours on end was tiring. The spit was heavy. The fire was hot. The lad had been up since well before dawn. But the only way to earn your keep in the castle kitchens was to do your job.

There were other lads more than willing to take on the task for the room and board that came with it. Tristan himself had cranked a spit for two years before working his way up through the ranks of the kitchens.

"Easson!" he snapped. "Look sharp!"

The lad bolted upright in wide-eyed panic and resumed turning the handle on the spit. Campbell, the older lad feeding the fire, leered at him.

"The queen's countin' on ye," Tristan chided.

"Aye, sir."

Tristan examined the four roasting geese, giving one of the legs a jiggle with his heat-callused fingers. The meat didn't appear to be burned. God willing, the fowl would be basted and succulent for dinner at midday, for the queen was counting on Tristan as well.

The baptism of Queen Mary's son on the morrow was to be the most significant event since her return to Scotland. She'd spared no expense, borrowing funds from the merchants of Edinburgh to pay the cost, which was rumored to be over twelve thousand pounds.

Originally, the baptism had been planned for October. But the queen had fallen ill—so ill that for a time it was feared she might die. By God's grace, she'd recovered, but further delays were caused by the conflicting schedules of the various ambassadors.

Meanwhile, the queen had moved the court three times. Tristan and the other cooks had packed and unpacked nearly two dozen carts of kitchen wares with each journey. Each location offered unique challenges. He'd never liked the layout of the kitchens at Craigmillar. And they'd hardly stayed long enough at Holyrood to lay a good fire.

At least they were home now. Tristan could find his way around the Stirling kitchens with his eyes closed. And, thanks to the master cook, Thomas Chalmers, the larders were well-stocked.

This morn, Tristan was making his usual rounds, supervising the kitchen staff. He nodded his approval of the blanched almonds and sampled a bite of custard. He stopped to dip his little finger into a pot of steaming ginger sauce for a quick taste.

At that moment, the master cook tromped into the

room, waving away the smoke as he shouted over his shoulder. "Ye fetch those eggs straightaway, Sinclair, or I'll show ye the back o' my hand!"

Tristan smirked. Thomas Chalmers was a full foot shorter than Tristan and about as round as he was tall. He was all bellow and no bite. In all the time Tristan had been an apprentice to the master cook, he'd never seen the man lay a hand on anyone.

Tristan closed his eyes to savor the gentle heat of ginger on his tongue. Then he spoke to young Chris Lamb, who was stirring the sauce. "Try a wee bit more salt."

"Aye, sir."

Thomas wiped his pudgy hands on his soiled apron. "Ah, MacKenzie, just the man I need."

Tristan straightened. He took pride in knowing he was the master cook's right-hand man.

"The waterways were closed again last night." Thomas paused to sample the ginger sauce himself. "We're short on trout for dinner. Who can ye spare to go fish in the firth?"

Tristan perused the room. Ten workers chopped and scalded, plucked and roasted, stirred and basted with practiced efficiency. He couldn't really spare any of them.

"I'll find someone," he promised.

Thomas smacked his lips, then murmured, "He's right, Chris, just a wee bit more salt." To Tristan he said, "We'll need half a dozen—about so big." He held his hands apart, indicating a good twelve inches. Then he snapped his fingers at Patrick Rannald, who was headed for the bakehouse. "Pattie! How many loaves o' pandemain can ye have for me by supper?" And he was off again.

Tristan sighed. All the kitchen lads were busy. He supposed he'd have to go to the firth himself.

"Bloody hell," he grumbled under his breath as he untied his apron and tossed it aside. "I'm a cook, not a fisherman."

But he couldn't very well refuse the master cook. He'd worked under Thomas Chalmers for five years in the *cuisine de common*, preparing meals for the castle. Now that there was a good chance Thomas would be promoted to the *cuisine de bouche*, cooking for the queen herself, Tristan stood in line for a promotion as well...if he could prove he was worthy.

And if his worth depended on fishing on a frosty morn when he'd much rather be overseeing the toasty kitchens, he supposed that was just the price he had to pay.

He bundled up in his woolen cloak, grabbed an empty basket, and hoisted the hefty fishing pole propped against the wall over his shoulder.

By the time he tromped down the hill to the firth, the sun had just begun to stretch its yellow fingers across the grassy braes of Stirling. Tristan's breath made plumes in the crisp air as he clambered down the muddy slope.

The banks of the firth were scarred from the clandestine activity of the last few nights. The reason for closing the waterways was supposed to be a secret. But word traveled fast among the staff of the castle. Everyone knew about the nightly shipments of guns and artillery from Edinburgh.

The renowned Bastian Pagez was the grand architect of the three-day baptism festivities. He'd assured everyone concerned that the munitions were only for visual effect. He'd devised such spectacles before in France, to enormous acclaim. But this was to be the first fireworks display ever orchestrated in Scotland.

Considering the amount of gunpowder that had been delivered, Tristan hoped it wouldn't be the last.

He took off his boots and stockings and rolled up his trews. Then he slipped into the shadows under the great stone bridge, where the trout tended to hide. He prayed this wouldn't take long. His stomach was growling. He'd neglected to grab a barley loaf from the bakehouse to break his fast.

Digging in the mud, he found a fat worm. He baited the hook and lowered the line into the murky depths of the firth. Then he waited.

And waited.

And waited.

# CHAPTER 2

ery Graham threw back the hood of her brown worsted cloak. She skipped down the road ahead of the others, smiling in delight at the breathtaking glen below. The wide silver ribbon of the Firth of Forth wound through the grassy expanse. Houses with smoking chimneys huddled together along the cobbled lanes. Steam rose from the wet stones and naked branches.

It was said that Stirling was like a giant kilt pin clasping together the Lowlands and the Highlands. Situated between the majestic peaks to the north and the rolling hills of the south, this expansive, wooded valley looked like a beautiful gem set into that pin. Especially this morn, where everything the sun touched turned to gold.

She glimpsed the castle on the far side of the firth and stopped to catch her breath. The imposing structure dominated everything around it. It appeared to be carved into the mountain. Its soft golden towers rose in stark contrast to the darker rock below, like heaven rising above hell. She couldn't wait to see what it looked like inside.

She glanced back along the road. What was taking everyone so long? True, the other minstrels were several years older than she was. They'd probably been to Stirling a dozen times. Still—for heaven's sake—they were going to perform for the new prince. Surely that deserved at least a little more enthusiasm.

This would be the second time she'd sung in the presence of Queen Mary. Three years ago, the minstrels had performed at the Campbell Castle for the wedding of the Earl of Argyll, where the queen had been a guest.

After their brilliant performance, they'd been invited to sing all over Scotland. Mery had sung in the households of Scottish nobles from Edinburgh to Inverness. But this would be the first time she'd performed for the queen in her home at Stirling Castle.

Again she glared back at her eight companions—four men, three women, and one packhorse—and shook her head. What dawdlers and woolgatherers they were this morn.

She couldn't wait for them any longer. Picking up her russet skirts, she swept down the road, descending to the great stone bridge that crossed the firth.

From the middle of the bridge, Stirling Castle looked even more impressive, rising up in regal splendor. It was a shame her kinfolk weren't here to see it.

None of the Grahams had ventured far from their Highland home of Nairn. They were simple folk with simple wants—peat for their fire, bread on their table, and fish in their nets. Her Da had made a decent living off of his boat. And her Ma had raised five upstanding sons who'd given her not a moment's worry.

And then Mery had come along.

For Mery, life was an adventure. Her Ma said she'd come out of the womb asking questions. Mery never walked when she could run. She never looked before she leaped. She was curious and fearless. Her Da claimed she was intrepid to a fault.

Her brothers knew there was almost nothing Mery wouldn't do on a dare. So naturally they'd encouraged her daring. She'd climbed the tallest tree in the village, stolen the neighbor's cattle, and ventured across frozen lochs, all at the prodding of her siblings.

Her parents despaired of ever taming her wild nature.

But Mery didn't want to be tamed. And she had no intention of being confined to Nairn. She had lofty dreams that were languishing in the remote fishing village. She didn't want to become a fisherman's wife. She didn't want to look at the same gray sky every day. She thirsted for something more—for music and art, culture and adventure. She longed to explore the wide world. She wanted to dance and sing and live.

Once, her Ma had confided in Mery that she too had had such dreams. She'd given up on them. And now she said it was too late.

But it wasn't too late for Mery. There was still time for her to seize the day. Her Ma had told her to trust her feelings. Her heart, she said, would never lead Mery astray.

So when Mery's Da informed her he'd chosen a husband for her and expected her to settle down and start popping out bairns, he shouldn't have been surprised when she ran away with the first band of traveling minstrels to pass through Nairn. He should have realized that holding Mery back from her destiny was as futile as keeping the firth from flowing to the sea.

With her Ma's blessing and, for propriety's sake, telling the minstrels a wee lie—that she wasn't a maiden, but a young widow—Mery had been following that destiny for four years now. The minstrels—Harry, Brian, Davy, Christopher, Elspeth, Anne, and Ginny—treated her like a cousin.

And what grand adventures Mery had had. Unafraid, she embraced each new experience with enthusiasm. She was a quick study, hungry to learn. She absorbed everything around her. It wasn't long before she was singing circles around her fellow minstrels.

Leaning over the stone wall of the bridge, she peered down into the water drifting lazily past. It was probably icy cold. Her brothers would have goaded her into jumping in. They were always getting her into trouble.

They were the ones who'd taught her that naughty song when she was a wee lass and dared her to sing it for her parents.

It had been a long time since she'd thought about that. It was a pretty song, an old song—*Quam pulchra es*—based on biblical text. But that text was the lusty Song of Solomon—wildly inappropriate words coming out of the mouth of a six-year-old lass.

Atop the water, a leaf floated toward her, passing under the bridge. As she crossed to watch it emerge again on the other side, the old song began to wind around her ears. Before long, she was humming it under her breath.

She closed her eyes and lifted her face to the winter sun, welcoming the meager warmth on her brow as she sang softly.

Opening her eyes again, she continued to sing, louder now, as she gazed at the awakening landscape and the distant empty streets of Stirling.

"*Et ubera tua botris,*" she sang to the firth. *Your breasts are like clusters of grapes.*

Since no one was about, she clapped one hand to her bosom and leaned over the bridge wall to serenade the water with heartfelt devotion.

When she got to the line, "*dilecte mi, egrediamur in agrum,*" *my beloved, let us go out into the fields,* she extended one arm in dramatic entreaty.

She was at full volume by the time she reached the lyrics, "*Ibi dabo tibi ubera mea,*" *there I will give you my breasts,* and had just taken a breath to belt out the last *alleluia* when a harsh bark from under the bridge interrupted her.

"Faith! Can ye not be quiet?"

She gasped and retreated in surprise from the edge.

"Ye're scarin' the fish," the man added in a growl.

At first, she was mortified. She hadn't expected anyone to be up and about at this time of day. She certainly hadn't meant for anyone to hear her...particularly considering the suggestive lyrics of that song.

But then she grew angry. Scaring the fish? What was that supposed to mean?

Clenching her fingers in her skirts and steeling her jaw, she approached the edge again. "Show yourself, sir," she demanded.

"What?"

"I said, show yourself. I'd like to see what manner o' cowardly troll hides under a bridge to insult passersby."

There was a pause. Then he yelled up, "I don't have time for this. Be off with ye."

Her eyes widened. "How dare ye!" She was truly livid now. The Highland brogue she usually tried to hide came out thick now. "Ye clearly dinna ken talent when ye hear it. I'll have ye know I'm on my way to sing for the queen herself."

That got his attention. He came out from under the bridge with his fists on his hips to stare up at her.

She instantly wished she'd left well enough alone.

The man was hardly a troll. In fact, he was striking enough to make her breath catch. He had messy chestnut hair, a square-jawed face, and a steely gaze. He was broad-shouldered, thick of forearm, and unapologetically manly, which was emphasized by the fact that his doublet was unfastened and his linen shirt untucked. His trews were rolled up to his knees. His muscular calves and feet were bare and flecked with mud. But despite his rumpled appearance and challenging glower, he was the most appealing man she'd ever seen.

Until he gave her a smoldering head-to-toe perusal and a cocky smile, and then opened his brazen mouth.

"And I'll have *ye* know I'm on my way to cook her dinner. The queen might be able to do quite well without the caterwaulin' of a lass, but she'll *starve* without *my* talents."

Mery's jaw dropped. Caterwauling? For once she was speechless.

He gave her a half chuckle and a dismissive wave. "Off ye go, lass."

She would have cut him to ribbons with her tongue then—no matter how attractive he was—but the rest of the minstrels had just alit on the bridge. She didn't want them to catch her in an altercation with one of the locals before they'd even been properly welcomed to Stirling.

So she sniffed and turned up her nose. Clutching her skirts in her fists, she stomped off across the bridge.

He was a cad to ruin her lovely mood. But she had more important things to think about. She consoled herself with the fact that if he was cooking the queen's dinner, that meant he worked in the bowels of the castle kitchens. She'd likely never see him again.

Oblivious to her rattled mood, Harry, the leader of the minstrels, arrived beside her. "Mery, lass, slow down. Ye'll miss all the best bits."

Mery forced herself to an obedient amble as they made their way up the steep path to the castle. But she was so distracted by her incident with the cursed fisherman that she hardly glanced up when they entered through the long tunnel of the north gate.

Suddenly she was within the outer close of Stirling Castle, where there was a flurry of activity. All around her, people rushed to and fro. Armed soldiers marched past. Builders hammered on a wooden framework. Servants carrying baskets and jugs scurried from building to building. A woman herded geese past a cart piled high with cloth. A young mother carried a wee bairn on one hip and boughs of holly on the other. An old gentleman hobbled on a cane beside his trusty hound.

Anne the alto gave Mery a nudge of her elbow and pointed to the sculptures set into the alcoves on the exterior of the great hall. "Do ye see the cherubs? Some o' them are musicians."

"Aye," Harry added, "and there's the old king himself." He nodded to a bearded statue at the upper corner of the building.

"Mm." Mery nodded. But her mind was elsewhere.

How could her singing possibly scare fish? They didn't even have ears, did they? It was nonsense.

Somehow amid the chaos, Mery managed to stay with the rest of the minstrels while Harry looked for the man in charge. Finally, they were invited to break their fast with bread and wine in the great hall.

Great hall was an understatement. It was the greatest hall Mery had ever seen. The room was enormous. Five fireplaces were necessary just to keep it warm. The arched ceiling of wooden beams rose above pale-colored walls slotted with large windows that let the light stream in. Tapestries depicting a unicorn hunt adorned the walls.

She wondered what the acoustics were like. In halls as large as this, the echo could either enhance the harmonies or distract the singers.

She longed to try out the sound, but now she was afraid to open her mouth. After all, she'd hate to frighten any more beasts.

The buttered bread offered to the minstrels was quite tasty, with a crispy crust and a soft middle. On the road, they usually had to make do with cheat bread made of coarse grain. But this was fine, white, fluffy manchet. She was certain the troll from under the bridge hadn't made it. No one so rough-hewn could bake such refined bread.

After breakfast, they returned to the outer close. There they met the queen's celebrated director of entertainment, Bastian Pagez. The Frenchman explained to them that they would be allowed to rehearse in the great hall later today. He said an English consort would be arriving on the morrow to accompany them for the banquet.

He went on to explain other tedious details. But Mery

quickly tired of listening. She'd always had a busy mind. It was hard for her to focus on just one thing. Harry would fill her in on what she missed anyway.

She wondered what kind of fish they were having for dinner. She hoped it was trout. She liked trout, though she didn't care much for pike, which was too bony, or bream, which had a muddy flavor.

She wondered which the queen preferred. Mery supposed she'd never know. It wasn't likely they'd be singing for her tonight, since the festivities didn't officially begin until the morrow. Besides, the queen probably dined alone in her chambers unless there was a…

Someone came striding across the courtyard, interrupting her thoughts.

It was him. The troll. He had a basket full of fish, and a fishing pole was slung over one brawny shoulder.

As if she'd called out to him, he turned his head toward her.

She glared at him.

He gave her a lazy grin and shook his head.

She must have made some sound to express her disgust then, for Pagez broke off abruptly and turned to her.

"You!" he snapped, clearly vexed by her inattention. "What is your name?"

She gulped. Though the troll was several yards away, she could still feel him staring at her as he slowed his step.

"Mery," she choked out.

"Mery what?"

"Mery Graham, sir."

"Well, Mery Graham, either you listen or you leave. I have no time for troublemakers."

"Aye, sir." Mery lowered her eyes.

The troll snorted in amusement and started to resume his travel.

Then Pagez turned on him as well. "You. Fisherman."

Mery looked up. A muscle ticked in the man's cheek.

"I'm not a fisherman," he grumbled. "I'm a cook."

"Even better." Pagez stroked his chin. "Put down the basket. Let me look at you."

Mery fought back a giggle.

The cook's eyes narrowed to angry slits as he complied. But of course, he wouldn't dare contradict the infamous Bastian Pagez, who answered directly to the queen.

"Turn around," Pagez said.

He did so reluctantly.

Mery decided the man's back side looked as fit as his front side. Apparently, so did Pagez.

"Perfect," he said. "You will serve as the lead satyr for the entertainment. I'm certain the master cook can spare you."

When she saw the displeased shock on the cook's face, Mery had to bite her lip to keep from bursting into laughter. It served him right, she figured, for being so rude to her this morn.


Tristan fumed all the way across the courtyard.

This was why he preferred the safe haven of the kitchens. Nobody ever bothered him while he lurked in the dim depths of the underground warren. Nobody even noticed him.

Now, because of that irksome lass, the queen's man had singled him out to perform for the court as a—what was it? The lead satyr? What the hell was a satyr?

Once in the roasting room, he propped the fishing pole against the wall and heaved the basket of fish onto the heavy table.

"Murray!" he barked. "Come clean these trout."

Then he hung up his cloak and glanced at the fire to make sure Easson was still awake and turning the spit.

Tristan thought again about the woman on the bridge. To be fair, it wasn't the fish who'd been disturbed by her voice. It was him. She'd completely ruined his focus with her beautiful singing. He didn't know what she was singing about. It was something in a foreign language. But it was as compelling—and distracting—as the song of a Siren.

Peering up at her from the firth, he'd been startled to discover the lass was just as beautiful as she sounded. And that was even more disconcerting.

Her hair was the color of dark, wild honey, and her skin was custard-smooth. Her lips reminded him of a rosy, ripe peach. Her wide, expressive eyes were as mysterious and complex as French wine. And her body...

A tight-laced stomacher circled her waist, pushing up her modest breasts until they looked like two small, perfect loaves of bread...soft, tender, delicious.

At the memory, he let out his breath on a low whistle.

Just like cooking, fishing was an activity that required concentration, and the winsome lass had destroyed his.

Tristan felt less rattled now—now that he was in his element. The kitchens were a man's domain. Life was simpler when no women were underfoot—women like that troublemaking Mery Graham.

In the male world of the kitchens, he could swear. He could sweat. Hell, he could take off his doublet if it got too hot.

Women complicated things.

It wasn't that he disliked women. He adored them. In fact, he owed his current position to a woman—his mother. After Tristan's father had been killed in the battle of Pinkie Cleugh, his mother—a French maidservant in the royal household—had landed Tristan the job of turnbrochie in the kitchens.

She'd worked tirelessly to make a life for herself and her six-year-old son. He'd worked his way up through the ranks of the kitchens, becoming a proper cook at eighteen.

It was his mother who'd convinced the master cook to let Tristan single-handedly prepare his first formal supper—a wedding feast at The Sheep Heid tavern in Musselburgh—for two of the queen's loyal subjects. And it was the success of that event that had earned him the respect of the master cook.

She'd finally worked herself into an early grave two years ago. But at least she'd remained alive long enough to see Tristan achieve a position of merit in the queen's household.

"Good, ye're back!" Thomas called out as he waddled into the room. "Have ye got the key to the spicery? The sparrows are stewin', but we need saffron for the sauce."

"Oh, aye," Tristan said, digging in the small satchel tied beneath his doublet.

He placed the key in Thomas's palm. Thomas handed him a chunk of barley bread.

"Eat, lad," he urged. "Ye can't cook a hearty meal on an empty stomach."

Tristan nodded his thanks and dug in. The bread was still warm from the oven and so moist and smooth, it didn't even need butter.

"By the way, we're expectin' a few stragglers for the late dinner," said Thomas. "A troupe o' players or somethin'—about a dozen extra mouths to feed."

"Minstrels," he grunted.

"Aye, that's them. See them fed, will ye?"

Frankly, Tristan would rather not. He had no wish to cross paths with that troublemaking lass again, not after the fool Pagez had made of him.

But the master cook had his hands full, preparing supper for the rest of the castle folk. Thomas had more important things to do than serve the entertainers a late dinner.

"O' course." Tristan swallowed a bite of bread and was about to check on the custards when he had a sudden thought. "Oh, Thomas, tell me somethin'."

"Aye?"

"What the devil is a satyr?"

# CHAPTER 3

Three hours later, Tristan stood at the great kitchen table, surveying the leftovers that remained from the main dinner. He rather enjoyed the creative challenge of salvaging what was left to feed the servants. With over three hundred castle folk eating at every meal, there was rarely a shortage of surplus food. Why throw it away when it might fill an empty belly?

To his satisfaction, there was plenty here for the serving staff, as well as twelve or so minstrels. The last bit of roast goose could be combined with the leek and onion pottage. Stir in a handful of oats, boil it up, and it would become a tasty stew.

A few barley loaves remained in the bakehouse. He'd slice, butter, and sprinkle them with parsley. That, accompanied by cups of hearty beer, would provide a filling meal for the guests.

But there also remained an assortment of sauces, roast trout, a few untouched custards, sugared dates, and gingerbread. And it seemed a shame to waste perfectly good food.

At least that was what he told himself.

But the truth was he welcomed any opportunity to show off his cooking skills. And a wee part of him wanted to prove to that snobbish minstrel lass that he wasn't—what had she called him?—a troll.

Damn it, she'd gotten the wrong impression of him. He was a highly respected cook, and he intended to prove it to her.

Rubbing his palms together, he reevaluated the table.

There were two decent-sized trout left. He could portion them out, season the filets with mace, cloves, pepper, and verjuice, enclose each serving within a quick pastry, and pop them in the bakehouse oven until they were golden and flaky.

If he crumbled the gingerbread into dishes, added a dollop of custard mixed with rosewater and chopped, sugared dates, then crowned the top with a drizzle of preserved orange syrup, he'd have a delicious sort of trifle to finish the meal.

He smiled in wicked satisfaction. By the end of dinner, he'd have that high-and-mighty Mery Graham eating out of the palm of his hand.


Mery drummed her fingers on the trestle table in the great hall. She was impatient to try out the sound of the cavernous chamber. But the minstrels had yet to sing a single note.

Bastian Pagez had spent the entire morning discussing every aspect of the next three days. Mery was thrilled to learn that the performers would be wearing costumes for the banquet on the final day. Everyone would be portraying some sort of mythical creature.

Mery was chosen to be a Nereid, one of Poseidon's daughters. The Nereids had such beautiful voices that their singing could lure men to their death. It was the perfect part for her, especially because it proved that her voice most certainly did *not* scare fish.

Besides, it was far better than playing a stupid satyr.

She bit back a grin as she remembered the crestfallen expression on the cook's face when he learned he was to be part of the spectacle. She'd almost felt sorry for him...almost.

After Pagez's lecture, the minstrels had been guided to their lodgings along the main esplanade of Stirling. The fine stone house where they were to stay was three stories high. Their host, an old soldier with a steel leg, welcomed them into his wife's spectacle shop on the ground floor. He then led them upstairs, past the middle floor, which featured a cozy hearth with comfortable seating and a modest kitchen. They were allowed to unpack their things in a pair of rooms on the top floor, which also housed at least six of the hosts' bespectacled children.

Now the minstrels had returned up the long hill to the castle. Mery was ravenous. Her stomach growled as she sat with the others at the table in the great hall. The denizens of the castle had already supped, which wasn't unusual. Minstrels and servants almost always ate before or after everyone else, since they normally sang during meals.

She didn't expect much more than thin pottage. So it was a pleasant surprise when a steaming bowl of hearty stew and a thick slab of barley bread were placed before her.

"I hope 'tis to your likin'," came a familiar voice.

Mery craned her head around. The cocksure rogue of a

cook stood behind her. Her heart skipped a beat at the sight of him, to her exasperation. After all, he was too ridiculously handsome for a common cook. He'd cleaned up, buttoned his doublet, and put his hair in order. He looked almost civilized.

At least he *did*...until she met his wicked, glittering gaze. Though he addressed the whole company of minstrels, his eyes were fixed on her. Mischief sparkled in the bright blue orbs, as if he issued her a challenge.

And because Mery had never been able to resist a challenge, she returned his bold smile. She raised a spoonful of pottage, prepared to give him her ruthlessly honest opinion.

Then she tasted it.

Delicious didn't begin to describe it. The vegetables were firm and flavorful, not boiled into oblivion, as was usually the case with stews. The bits of roast goose lent a smoky aroma to the dish. She tasted leeks, onions, parsley, and pepper—strong, but not overpowering. Mery closed her eyes to relish the flavor.

She wasn't the only one impressed. All around her, the minstrels oohed and ahhed over the rich stew.

Harry was the first to speak. "Give my compliments to the cook, lad. I believe this is the best pottage I've ever had."

"Thank ye," the cook replied with a nod of his head.

Anne the alto gasped. "Faith, did ye make this?" she asked.

"I did."

"Well, 'tis superb. Isn't it superb, Brian?"

Brian the tenor nodded his head. "Mmm."

Davy the bass chimed in. "And the barley bread! 'Tis as soft and supple as a harlot's—"

"Davy!" chided Isabel, the other alto.

Davy grinned.

He was right about the barley bread. It was divine.

But Mery wasn't much inclined to rave over the cooking of a man who'd insulted her singing, no matter how handsome he was.

Still, it didn't keep her from eating every last crumb.

"And for the next course…" the cook announced.

The minstrels gave a collective gasp of pleasure. They were unaccustomed to being served more than one course.

The cook continued with a smile. *"La truite en croûte."* He bent down slightly, murmuring for her benefit, as if she couldn't speak French perfectly well, "Trout in a crust."

She stiffened. "I ken what it is." She resisted adding that apparently her singing hadn't scared away the trout after all.

While everyone carried on over the darling little flaky golden pouches filled with trout, Mery tried not to enjoy the rest of her pottage.

She meant to leave her *truite en croûte* untouched. The last thing she wanted to do was to reward the efforts of the swaggering lout of a cook.

Unfortunately, she was still hungry. So while he wasn't looking, she broke off a small piece and nibbled at it. It was quite good. The pastry was buttery and light.

She took a bigger bite. The trout was so fresh, she could taste the clean, bracing flavor of the firth in it.

One more bite, and the delicate spices of mace and clove swirled over her tongue.

Just as she was about to take a fourth taste, the cook leaned down. "I can take that away if ye don't like it."

"Nae," she blurted, gripping her plate in panic before he could remove it.

He flashed an irritating grin, clearly trying to provoke her. "So ye *do* like it."

She gave him a casual shrug, just to annoy him.

"Ye're a stubborn lass," he whispered.

She whispered back, "I willna be courteous to a man who insulted my voice."

"Ah."

"I'll have ye know that voice earned me the role of a Nereid for the banquet."

It wasn't quite true. Bastian Pagez hadn't even heard her sing yet. He'd chosen her on appearance alone. But the cook didn't have to know that.

"A Nereid?" the cook murmured.

She arched a smug brow. "And a Nereid is a great deal more respectable than a satyr."

# CHAPTER 4

Tristan scowled. He still didn't know what a satyr was. Nobody in the kitchens seemed to know. He'd never heard of a Nereid either. But he wasn't about to admit his ignorance to the saucy maid with the sparkly eyes.

He bent to whisper against her hair, "Ye know, between ye and me, 'tis unwise to be on bad terms with the man cookin' your food."

She gave a tiny, satisfying gasp, glancing suspiciously at the remains of her trout.

"Don't worry, I haven't poisoned ye," he said. "Yet."

He didn't know why, but he found perverse pleasure in ruffling the sassy lass's feathers just a wee bit.

He moved on then to the other guests, who raved over the trout. From the corner of his eye, he watched the lass poke at her fish, sigh, and finally resign herself to finishing it. He also saw the satisfaction in her face as she licked the last morsel from her dainty fingers. And that did strange things to his insides.

When the minstrels finished their dinner, he had the

trifles brought out. As he predicted, none of the guests had ever seen such a concoction. Tristan considered the trifle one of the few brilliant English inventions. The layered sweet was so new and uncommon in Scotland, and there were so many variations of it, a cook could use almost any ingredients and dub it a trifle.

The minstrels and the servants, for whom the extravagant sweet was a rare treat, began extolling its virtues. But though it was gratifying to hear their compliments, he found he was mostly interested in what the Highland lass thought of it.

He watched her from across the table as she took a tentative taste. She rolled her eyes in ecstasy, licked her lips, and went for another bite.

Why that pleased him, Tristan didn't know. But his heart beat faster when he saw the genuine delight in her face.

It wasn't often he received praise. The nobles of Stirling had a spoiled palate and were accustomed to fine food. Dining on delicacies like orange syrup, rosewater, and sugared dates was nothing special for them.

Preparing food for people who sincerely appreciated it was far more rewarding. And if Mery Graham started appreciating it any more sincerely, he thought as she closed her eyes and ran the tip of her delicate tongue around the edge of her exquisite lips...

The breath left his lungs as he continued to observe her. A powerful surge went through his loins as he she savored every velvety bite. He didn't realize he was scowling until she glanced up at him, her brow furrowed in puzzlement.

Snatching up the nearest cup of ale, he downed it in one gulp, ignoring the protests of the maidservant to whom it belonged.

It didn't help.

Perhaps he should have poured the ale down his trews.

Lately, he'd been too busy to pay much heed to the neglected beast in his breeches. But now it seemed to be roaring in demand.

Why the lass should affect him so, he couldn't fathom. Aye, she was bonnie. But the court was full of bonnie lasses.

Nae, there was something different about this one—her spirit, her wit, her temper, or maybe the way she'd stood up to him on the bridge—that fired his blood and made his senses go awry.

She finished her trifle before everyone else. He passed behind her to collect her empty bowl.

"So did ye enjoy your poison?" he teased.

She smirked. "Ye wouldn't dare poison the lass who's to play a Nereid for the queen."

"Oh, *I* wouldn't, but a satyr might."

"Then ye'd best beware, satyr." She nodded to the last tapestry on the wall, which depicted the killing of a trapped unicorn. "Ye can see what the royals do to unicorns."

Tristan narrowed his eyes at the tapestry. Maybe a satyr was similar to a unicorn.

She clucked her tongue. "Why would they wish to kill such a beautiful beast?"

"A unicorn?" he quipped, removing her bowl and giving her a sly wink. "They're delicious."

Her jaw fell open, and she swatted him.

Tristan was grinning like a fool all the way back to the kitchens. What fun the lass was. Though he casually bedded his share of willing women, he didn't speak much with them. The few times he tried, his dark and biting remarks usually escaped their understanding.

But Mery Graham had instantly seen the humor in his words. Her eyes had registered at first shock, and then amusement. And when she cuffed him, it felt as if she knocked his brains a bit askew.

Here was a woman who gave as good as she got. In the world of courtly protocol, it was refreshing to address a lass who spoke her mind. If only all women were so forthright and outspoken, he might actually consider pursuing one.

As he ducked back into the kitchens, he was in such good spirits that he didn't even bark at Easson, who was now napping by the dying coals. Instead, he gave the fire a few jabs to keep it going for the next round of roasting and let the lad sleep.

The rest of the day, while he supervised the stewing of hens, the simmering of pottages, and the blending of sauces, he couldn't get Mery Graham out of his mind.

He kept wondering what she would think of this sauce or that custard, whether she would prefer the apple or pear tarts. The delectable vision of Mery licking her lips as she dined on his dishes was never far from his thoughts.

The master cook was busier than usual, which meant Tristan rarely stopped to take a breath. He knew Thomas was counting on him to work side-by-side with him, to make sure nothing slipped through the cracks. Not only did they have to orchestrate and serve a three-day event for scores of nobles, but they had to ensure the rest of the castle folk were fed. The royals might take precedence, but it was vital that no one in the household go hungry.

It was late afternoon when Campbell passed through the kitchen corridor with a tray full of cups.

"What's that?" Tristan asked.

"Ale, sir," the lad replied.

"Where are ye bound?" Tristan asked.

"The great hall, sir."

Tristan furrowed his brows. He kept a close watch on the provisions. Nothing left the kitchens without the express permission of Thomas Chalmers or himself.

"Who ordered them?"

"Master Thomas. He said I was to take drink to the minstrels."

On impulse, Tristan tore off his apron and took the tray from Campbell. "I'll take that. Meanwhile, see if ye can find a jar o' quince preserves in the stores."

"Aye, sir."

Tristan ascended from the kitchens, shaking his head, marveling at the lengths to which he'd apparently go to glimpse that minx of a minstrel once more.

He heard them before he saw them. Angels. At least they sounded like angels. Harmonies as soft, sweet, and light as whipped cream snow filled the great hall, spilling into the passage.

For a moment, he paused at the doorway, trying to decipher which voice was Mery's. It was impossible. The voices mingled so flawlessly that he couldn't tell where one ended and another began. The playful notes floated and danced, skipped and turned, and then tumbled into a merry jumble.

Toiling in the kitchens, he didn't often get to listen to the entertainment. He'd heard performers at the spring fair. But they'd sounded nothing like this.

The song was incredibly complex. The minstrels' contrasting voices—bright, mellow, delicate, sharp—were like expertly measured spices that blended together to create a unique and tasty dish.

Indeed, the music was so captivating that he couldn't bear to interrupt the song. He closed his eyes, letting the beautiful echoes wash over him.

He didn't understand the lyrics. They sounded Italian. But the song seemed to be lighthearted in tone. It probably wasn't about hunting unicorns.

The music began to slow. The minstrels held out the final note, which echoed in the great hall. And then the magic of the moment was broken by the leader of the minstrels.

"Elspeth, ye were a wee bit sharp on that high note again. And Brian, ye're still rushin' the line before the last verse. Try to stay with Chris."

Tristan quietly cleared his throat to announce his arrival.

"At last!" one of the men exclaimed.

"Just in the nick o' time," said another, winking, "before Harry could make us sing that infernal tune one more time."

Harry replied with a laugh. "Well, if ye'd sing it right the first time..."

The eight of them rushed up to Tristan, snatching ales from the tray. He was startled to hear them belittling the music. To him, it had sounded heavenly.

He felt the brush of skirts against his leg.

"What have ye brought us?" asked a silky voice beside him.

Unable to resist the jest, he murmured, "Unicorn piss."

She jabbed him in the ribs with her elbow, almost making him drop the tray. Then she took a cup of ale and proceeded to swig it down all at once.

He raised a brow.

She sniffed defensively. "Singin' is thirsty work."

He gave her a half grin. "Want another?"

She hesitated.

"Go on," he urged.

She cast about furtively, then took another cup, muttering, "Harry will have my head if I'm in my cups for the next song." She nonetheless took a healthy gulp.

"What's the next song?"

She thought for a moment, then almost spit out her ale on a giggle. "'Tis a drinkin' song."

He chuckled along. In that instant of shared laughter, he felt a strong and curious attraction to her.

It was absurd. Tristan wasn't a man ruled by his heart. Running the kitchens required thought and attention to detail. There was no room in his head or time in his busy day to pay heed to every bonnie lass that passed by.

Besides, he'd only just met Mery Graham. All he knew about her was that she had a prickly nature, a fiery temper, and a penchant for ale. She was likely a widow or at least a woman of questionable morals to be traveling alone with minstrels. She also had soft green eyes, an adorable pout, and a body to drive a man mad. But there was something more about her—something wild and spirited—that heated his blood.

"So how did ye happen to fall in with this company?" he asked, nodding to the minstrels.

She arched a brow at him. "Well, I was out scarin' fish one day..."

He grimaced. He deserved that. Indeed, he was about to apologize for his rudeness when the leader of the minstrels clapped his hands to summon the singers.

She downed the rest of her ale and placed the empty cup on his tray. He would have said more. But with a whirl of her scarlet skirts, she swept off, leaving behind only her flowery, feminine scent.

Tristan lingered long enough to hear the beginning of the drinking song, which compared the virtues of wine and women.

He watched Mery sing. Her face seemed to come to life. Her eyes lit up. Her dimples deepened. Her lips curved into a flirtatious smile.

So captivated was he by her expressions and the merry play of the music, he almost forgot that he'd left a sorrel sauce simmering on the fire.

Cursing his inattention, he withdrew from the hall and loped back to the kitchens. He arrived just in time to see a scowling Thomas stirring the abandoned sauce.

# CHAPTER 5

No matter how hard Mery tried to focus on the rehearsal, she couldn't stop thinking about that infernal cook. Zounds, she didn't even know the man's name. She certainly shouldn't be attracted to him. In fact, she shouldn't give him any thought whatsoever. He obviously had no ear for music. He had yet to apologize for insulting her. And he poked fun at her at every opportunity.

True, he was rather witty. She had a soft spot for anyone who could make her laugh. He had a wry grin, dazzling blue eyes, and hair she'd love to run her fingers through. As for his wide shoulders and powerful arms...well, they made her heart flutter in the most odd...

"Mery!" Harry barked.

She jumped.

"Ye missed your entrance," he scolded.

"Did I?"

She *had* to stop thinking about him. This was going to be the most important performance of her life. She had to be at her best.

They began the song again. This time, Mery focused intently on her part.

After all, if the minstrels sang well enough, Queen Mary might ask them to return. She might even ask them to stay at Stirling, to be her court musicians. Mery's future depended on delivering a brilliant performance. She had to think about every note. She couldn't let a pair of twinkling eyes and a firm and manly backside distract her from...

"Mery!"

"What!" she snapped back.

"The word is 'sweeter,' her lips are 'sweeter'."

"I know the words!" She furrowed her brow. "Wait. What did I sing?"

"'Satyr'?"

Anne the alto snickered.

Mery bit her lip. "I won't do it again."

Damn that cook! She would forget about him. She *would.*

Her plan worked for the next two songs. But in the middle of *Toutes les Nuitz,* when they started singing about a woman missing her lover beside her in bed, the cook's handsome face suddenly sprang to mind. And when she got to the phrase, *au lieu de vostre bouche en soupirant je baise l'oreiller, in place of your mouth I kiss the pillow,* she grew short of breath, wondering how his smug mouth would taste, and she ran out of air before the end of the line.

She decided she had to finish the matter once and for all. She had to confront the cook. What she'd do, she didn't know. She'd have to follow her instincts. But if she hoped to make this performance a success, she had to purge the fascinating, infuriating man from her thoughts.

Her next opportunity came hours later, at dinner.

A smaller meal was served to the minstrels and two dozen various household servants shortly after the main dinner for the nobles. Though Mery kept eyeing the entrance of the hall, the cook never came through it. Kitchen lads brought in the first course—roast capons with a sweet wine sauce, wee mutton pies, and a lovely custard with raisins.

There was a brief respite between the first and second courses. It was then Mery made her move.

She told Harry she needed to be excused for a moment. Then she slipped out. She crossed the small bridge that connected the great hall and the kitchens and crept onward, guided by the alluring scent of roasting meats.

The passageway grew warmer and the plaster walls more smoke-blackened as she descended the stairs. She heard shouting farther down, accompanied by the banging of pots and the clatter of cutlery.

All at once, a kitchen boy collided with her. His eyes went wide, and he nearly dropped his basket of bread. He mumbled an apology and quickly juggled the loaves back into the basket, then continued down the passageway, giving her a curious backward glance as he headed toward the great hall.

She rounded the corner where the smoke was thicker. It looked like a beehive. Workers were crowded into the tight quarters. Lads with steaming platters and sizzling spits hurried to and fro, yelling out orders and elbowing their way past each other.

The lad closest to her gave a yelp and backed against the wall as if she were some demon who'd suddenly materialized before him. She frowned and picked up her skirts to sidle past him.

For a moment, she forgot her purpose, fascinated by the activity going on around her. She'd never seen proper kitchens before.

Burly cooks sweated over enormous cauldrons. Wee boys with ash-covered faces turned spits as long as lances. Red-faced men with beefy arms whipped up frothy sauces in bowls. Scrawny lads balancing eggs and bundles of herbs squeezed between them.

Their movements seemed as carefully composed as a madrigal. Each worker followed his own path, which wove through the others, brilliantly intersecting without clashing and creating disharmony.

And the smells—savory roasts, spicy sauces, fresh-baked bread, honey, pepper, mustard—made her mouth water.

A lad carrying a jug spied her, froze, and turned around to go back the way he'd come. He whispered something to one of the older cooks, who frowned until the lad pointed at her. Then the older cook straightened, and his frown deepened.

Mery, sensing she should hurry along, slipped out of sight behind a man who was furiously chopping onions. She proceeded along the long wooden table in the middle of the room, brushing past men peeling leeks, slicing parsnips, and tearing greens.

When she bumped into a man quartering turnips, he swung around with a scowl and a giant knife. His brows shot up when he saw her.

Eyeing his blade with mistrust, she mumbled an apology and continued on. But by now, everyone in the kitchens had noted her presence.

One by one, the workers ground to a halt. The spoons

ceased stirring. The knives went quiet. The spits stopped turning. All eyes swiveled to her in alarm.

In the midst of the silence, the very man Mery was seeking backed into the room with a yell. "Easson, give the hare's leg a jiggle! See if 'tis—" He stopped when he realized he was shouting. He halted, studying the room in consternation.

Mery gulped.

Here, in his element, the cook looked magnificent. He had the voice of authority and the confidence of a king.

Her gaze roved shamelessly over his body. He'd removed his doublet. His pale shirt was rolled up to the elbows, exposing his muscled forearms, and open at the top, which revealed the vee of his chest. A stained white apron was tied around his waist. The sheen of sweat glazed his brow and darkened strands of his hair. His eyes were deep and mysterious...and narrowed at her in disapproval.

The men looked at him, waiting to see what he would do.

"What the devil?" he said. "What are *ye* doin' here?"

Their gaze returned to Mery, awaiting her reply.

She lifted her chin. She might feel out of place here. But she wasn't about to let a room full of kitchen boys intimidate her. "Lookin' for *ye*, if ye must know."

"Me? Well, ye can't just..." He glanced around the room and set his fists on his hips. "What are ye lads gawkin' at? Don't ye have work to do?"

The men resumed their tasks at once. He made his way toward her, whipping off his apron to wipe his hands on it before he grabbed her by the elbow.

He started to tug her away—rather roughly, she thought. It was only natural that she resist.

He tugged her again.

She tugged back.

"What are ye doin?" he muttered. "Ye need to get out o' here."

"Stop yankin' on me."

"I'm not..." He let out a sound of exasperation. "Fine," he said, letting go of her. "Will ye come this way, my lady?" he asked, sketching a mockery of a bow before he slapped the apron over his shoulder.

She closed down her eyes in a simmering glare, but followed him up a narrow set of steps. They led to a small chamber that was considerably cooler than the roasting room.

When she spied the assortment of sweets lining the wooden shelf along one wall, Mery's eyes went round. Her irritation was instantly forgotten. The air smelled divine, like honey, cream, almonds, and cinnamon.

"What *is* this place?" she asked in wonder.

"The confectionary." He wadded his apron into a pile on the counter. "Now, look, lass, ye can't be strollin' into the kitchens—"

"The confectionary?" She stepped closer to the shelf, pointing to a row of jewel-like sweets. "What are those?"

"Those? Marchpane. Now, lass—"

"They look like stained glass," she gushed.

"I suppose so. Listen to me. This is no place for a—"

"And these?" she asked, her attention caught by the perfect golden squares topped with bright yellow syrup and red currants.

"Tablet with quince preserves. Nae! Don't touch them. They're for the nobles."

She withdrew her hand. She'd only wanted a closer look. He didn't have to shout at her. "Is this...?"

"Blancmange."

She loved blancmange. The almond cream didn't appear to be quite set yet, which was just the way she liked it—soft and as smooth as silk.

"What about these?" she asked, dropping down to eye level to examine the fluffy white dollops that looked like drifts of snow.

He sighed. "Meringues."

"Oh, my. How did ye make them?"

"If I tell ye, will ye leave me alone and go back to the hall?"

She straightened, frowning in disappointment. "Ye *are* a mean old troll."

"Listen, I can't have a lass sniffin' around my kitchens."

She would have gasped at his rude behavior, but her attention was drawn to an amazing sculpture at the end of the shelf. It was a beautiful replica of Stirling Castle all in white, decked with colored flags and painted with the carved crest of Queen Mary.

"Ooooh, what's this?"

He testily crossed his arms. "I'm sure ye've seen a subtlety before."

Of course she had. They put subtleties on the table to introduce every important banquet. "None this fabulous. It looks...delicious." She tapped her fingers on the edge of the shelf, tempted to break off a piece of the sugar parapet.

"Don't even think of it, lass," he warned, as if he'd read her mind.

"Fie!" She gave him a disgruntled pout. "Mean *and* stingy."

"I don't think the queen would appreciate ye layin' siege to her castle."

He was probably right. But there were lots and lots of other sweets. Nobody would notice if one or two of them went missing. She tucked her lower lip under her teeth, wishing she could taste just one.

Half amused and half exasperated, the cook finally let out a rueful chuckle of surrender. "If I give ye a sweet, will ye go on your merry way then?"

She couldn't help the gleam that came into her eyes. "Only one?"

He shook his head in self-mockery. "Fine. Two. But then ye have to go. The kitchens are no place for a woman."

She raised a brow at that, and then perused the selection. It would be hard to choose just two. Finally, she pointed to a piece of the quince tablet.

He picked it up and placed it in her palm.

She popped it into her mouth, and closed her eyes in joy. "Mmmm."

The texture of the rich, sugary square was like fine sand, yet it melted to a velvety finish in her mouth. The sweet syrup of the quince preserves balanced perfectly with the tart bite of the red currants. She licked her lips and smiled.

When she opened her eyes to slits again, he was staring at her mouth. What she glimpsed in his smoky gaze was enough to make her want to forego the second sweet and sample the cook instead.

# CHAPTER 6

Tristan felt a current of desire go through him as he watched the lass taste the quince tablet. It had been a long while since he'd seen anyone take such blatant sensuous pleasure in food.

But in the more sensible part of his brain, he knew he couldn't afford to linger here, watching her lick quince juice off of her fingers, no matter how it made his pulse throb. Women didn't belong in the kitchens. If Thomas saw her...

"Ye need to go," he choked out. That wasn't what his body was telling him. But he forced the words from his lips.

She glanced at him with a creased brow and an endearing pout. "But ye promised I could have two."

There was no disguising the calculating glimmer in her eyes. But even knowing he was being manipulated, he couldn't refuse her. "Aye, fine, but make haste."

Her second selection was a meringue. She bit into it, and her eyes widened as it dissolved on her tongue.

Tristan couldn't help but smile. Meringues of egg whites—whipped up to a weightless froth, sweetened, then stiffened over a low fire to hold their shape—resulted in a confection as light and insubstantial as air.

"'Tis like takin' a bite of a cloud," she cooed as her tongue slipped out to lick a sticky crumb from her lip.

The mischievous lass was as tempting as the sweets. He'd like to have licked that crumb from her lip himself.

Then he gave his head a shake. This was the eve of the most important event of his life. He truly had no time for distractions like Mery Graham.

"Go on with ye now," he said.

"Why?" she replied, sucking the sweetness from her fingertip.

The gesture made a twinge go through his groin. "Why what?"

"Why do I have to go?"

Marry, he wished she didn't. "I told ye. Women don't belong in the kitchens."

"But why?"

Leave it to the outspoken lass to ask him such a thing. She frowned at him as if *he'd* made the decree. But the kitchens had *always* been the domain of men. They were hot and smoky places, full of heavy iron cauldrons and massive joints of beef. What woman would *want* to venture there?

This one, apparently.

"Because they ask too many questions," he replied, crossing his arms over his chest again and eyeing her roving fingers. "And get your thievin' paws away from the sweetmeats."

She gasped, recoiling as if he'd swatted her hand.

He shook his head. "I swear, if I let ye stay here any longer, there'll be nothin' left for the queen."

She cocked her chin and gave him a pretty pout. "Well, if they weren't quite so temptin', I wouldn't..."

He heard footsteps on the stairs. His first ridiculous instinct was to protect the lass. He set her behind him, then whirled about with closed fists and a menacing scowl to face whoever was coming.

"MacKenzie!"

Bloody hell. It was the master cook.

"Aye?" he replied as Thomas entered the confectionary.

Thomas's eyes didn't miss a thing. "What the...what are ye doin' in the confectionary?" he demanded. Then his scowl darkened. "And why is there a lass stickin' her fingers in the blancmange?"

Tristan turned to glare at the lass, who looked as guilty as the devil.

She answered before he had a chance, raising her haughty chin. "I'm verifyin' the quality o' the sweets," she declared. "After all, we're not just *any* troupe o' minstrels. I'll have ye know we've performed all o'er Scotland, from Inverness to—"

"Lass!" Tristan interjected before her unwitting insults could turn the master cook's face any redder. "We may as well tell him the truth."

"The truth?" she asked.

"Aye." He scrambled for an excuse that Thomas would accept. "The lass... Mery... She's..." he said, flushing at the lie. "We're lovers."

"What?" Thomas said with an incredulous frown.

"What?" Mery said with an incredulous laugh. "That's the most—"

Before she could call him a liar, further slight the master cook, get the entire troupe of minstrels banned from Stirling, and possibly lose Tristan his position in the kitchens, he did the only reasonable thing to salvage the awkward situation.

He hauled Mery Graham into his arms and kissed her.

Kissing wasn't new for Mery. She'd been stealing kisses since she was twelve. So her first instinct wasn't necessarily to fight him.

It wasn't her second instinct either.

And the longer the kiss went on, the less she thought about fighting him at all.

Indeed, the sensation was quite pleasant. She could taste subtle, spicy ginger on his lips. She felt the masculine stubble that peppered his chin and heard his rasping breath against her cheek. Even the smoky smell of him was enticing.

She let her hands drift up along the line of his jaw. Slowly, she weaved her fingers into his thick hair. It was as soft and luxurious as she'd imagined. Tilting her head, she parted her lips, encouraging him to trespass there.

He seemed more than willing to oblige. He clasped the side of her neck with one powerful hand, pulling her firmly against him with the other. He surged forward with his demanding mouth. She felt, rather than heard, the soft, hungry growl deep in his throat.

She forgot all about their witness as she was swept up in the moment. Passion swirled around her like an ethereal harmony, carrying her along in its lofty embrace and conveying her heavenward.

Swiftly, before she could stem the tide, the kiss took on an intensity all its own. He dragged her even closer to him until her breasts were mashed against his chest. Like a starving beast, he devoured her.

Her knees grew weak, and a current of hot need shot through her body. Suddenly she wanted to do more than just kiss him.

"MacKenzie!"

MacKenzie abruptly broke off the kiss.

Mery staggered backward. She might have fallen had he not caught her shoulders. To her amazement, he looked as shocked as she was.

The intruder spoke. "Look, lad, I don't begrudge ye a wee *entremet* between courses." He raised his thick brows above his sweaty, round face as he gave her a quick perusal. "I'd even commend ye on your taste." Then he shook his head. "But ye're my right hand. Next time wait until supper is o'er."

MacKenzie—she still didn't know his first name—released her and lowered his hands. "'Twon't happen again," he grimly vowed.

Mery just as grimly vowed, if she had anything to say about it, it *would* happen again. The sharp-tongued rogue of a cook might ruffle her feathers a bit. But he also heated her blood in the loveliest way.

The other man wiped his hands on the apron tied around his big belly. "By my troth, why would ye bring her here, to the stinkin' bowels o' the kitchens?" He wagged a fat finger at Mery. "'Tis no place for a lass!" Then he muttered to MacKenzie, "Could ye not find a more romantic spot for a tryst, lad? God 'a mercy, ye're half French." He turned to leave, barking over his shoulder, "Get her out o' here! I can't have her upsettin' the kitchen staff!"

After he was gone, MacKenzie planted his hands sternly on his hips. "That," he growled, "is why ye shouldn't be in the kitchens."

His quiet snarl reminded her of a hostile hound. But she wasn't fooled. He might be barking now. But a moment ago...

Her eyes smoldered as she ignored his stormy brow and relived his delicious kiss, sweeter than anything lining the shelves of the confectionary.

He frowned at the floor. "Look, lass. I'm sorry I...I took such liberties with ye. That was the master cook. 'Twas the only thing I could think to do."

Mery wasn't listening. The corner of her lip lifted into a weak smile. She wasn't sorry in the least. Indeed, her mind was spinning, cataloguing the intriguing options that surrounded them.

"Kiss me again," she whispered.

He looked up. "What?"

She moved forward, dipping an errant finger into the blancmange. With her other hand, she clutched the front of his shirt and pulled him close. His expression was stony as she smeared the creamy liquid across her lips. When she would have painted his mouth as well, he seized her wrist to stop her.

But his nostrils flared, and his lips parted. And when his gaze lowered to her mouth, she knew they were both past temptation.

# CHAPTER 7

Tristan didn't know what was wrong with him. He shouldn't have kissed the lass the first time. It was only desperation that had driven him to it. And it had completely scrambled his brain.

He most definitely shouldn't kiss her a second time. There were a thousand reasons against it.

At the moment, however, he couldn't think of a damned one.

Her alluring smile, her foggy gaze, and the milky glaze of blancmange upon her lips made his reaction swift and strong. He could no more resist kissing her than he could resist stirring a pot of burning broth.

Catching her wrist had been futile. When she drew near, he tightened his grip on her arm, but he couldn't keep her at bay.

Nor did he much want to.

To be honest, he didn't know which of them actually initiated the second kiss. Somehow their mouths met—his flavored with desire, hers with sweet blancmange. Their hands tangled in each other's hair. He longed to bring her closer, to taste her more deeply, to swirl her essence over his tongue like a delicate sauce.

She gasped against his lips and opened to him, granting him access to the soft inner recesses of her mouth. Her fingers explored him with unabashed eagerness, skimming his throat, his shoulders, his chest.

Like a white-hot poker thrust into water, her touch brought him instantly to a boil. Need flared in him as a lightning bolt of desire shot from his buzzing ears to a place deep within his loins.

Too overcome with lust to temper his demands, he enclosed her in his arms, pressing her back against the plaster wall. Yet she made no attempt to escape the prison of his embrace. Instead, she moaned softly against his mouth, as if this was exactly what she desired.

He squeezed his eyes shut as her bold fingers drifted down his chest, grazing his ribs, slipping across his stomach. He held his breath as she trespassed dangerously low, close to where his arousal was alarmingly apparent.

And then a cursed serving lad burst into the room with a yell. "Blancmange!"

Tristan separated from Mery faster than oil from verjuice. He was sure guilt was written all over his flushed face, never mind what loomed large inside his trews.

Young Campbell looked mortified when he saw Tristan in the confectionary, even more mortified to discover his master was with a lass. The serving lad stammered out an apology, his eyes darting back and forth between the two of them.

Tristan straightened with purpose, dusted his hands together, and let out a decisive breath. He had to take control, clear things up, and get Mery out of here before the two of them became fodder for gossip.

"The blancmange is there." He nodded to the bowl. "And don't forget the pot o' honey glaze."

Campbell stared down at the bowl, his forehead creased in confusion. Tristan followed his gaze.

The blancmange was a mess. Mischievous Mery had gouged holes in the half-set dish. What had once resembled a pristine snowfield now looked as if it had been trampled by cattle.

"Here," Tristan decided, reaching for a loaf of gingerbread. He crumbled it apart over the blancmange. Then he swept up a dozen preserved cherries and placed them in a star pattern across the top. Finally, he took the pot of honey glaze and poured it in a thin criss-crossing ribbon over the top. "Tell them 'tis a trifle."

"Aye, sir." Campbell carried off the great bowl.

If they were already serving the third course, the confectioner would return soon. More lads would be coming to fetch sweets.

"Ye have to go now, lass," he urged Mery.

His heart, however, wasn't in bidding her adieu. He'd much rather loiter here, kissing the beautiful maid whose sweet lips rivaled anything in the confectionary.

By her expression, she was in agreement. She gave him a conspiratorial smile. "When shall we meet again, and where?"

He blinked. That he hadn't expected. What they'd done had been a mistake, a reckless, impulsive gesture, no more.

"I'm not sure we should," he said.

She chuckled. "Oh, aye, ye are." The cheeky lass actually

lowered her eyes then to the place he least wished her to look. "Ye're most certainly sure."

Tristan almost choked on chagrin. Now he was positive they shouldn't meet again. It would be too easy for him to fall prey to the tempting lass's feminine wiles, to succumb to her seduction, and for both of them to do things they would regret.

"Look, lass," he said, grabbing up his crumpled apron and wrapping it again around his waist, hiding the evidence of his arousal. "Maybe we should just forget what happened here." He tied the apron strings with a decisive yank.

She lifted a brow. "Well, 'twasn't *my* idea to claim we were lovers." She heaved a sigh full of false dismay. "Now it seems we're trapped in the lie."

He tried not to laugh. The lass was incorrigible. What a handful she must be for the leader of the minstrels. "Hardly trapped. Ye'll be leavin' in three days."

"That means we don't have much time." She gave him a wink. "So when can I see ye again?"

A foolish part of him truly *did* want to see her again. The lass was breathtaking, mouthwatering, and heart-throbbing. He wanted to feed her sweets, devour her mouth, and hold her close to him.

Indeed, he half convinced himself that he should hoist the white flag and succumb to his desires. Perhaps if he took his fill of her, it would be easier to walk away.

But this was the most important event in all of Scotland. He was the second in command of the kitchens. He had to remember his responsibilities to the master cook, to his queen, and to his country.

So he turned to her with as stern a frown as he could

muster. "Lass, ye heard the master cook," he said in the schooled rumble that made the kitchen lads scurry to do his bidding. "Ye need to go. Now."

Despite his warning growl, the lass behaved as if he were some adorable pup she wished to adopt.

"Oh, fine," she said on a less than compliant sigh. "But since we're 'lovers' now, I think ye owe me just one more thing."

One more thing. What could she mean? Another sweet? A farewell kiss? Something more? He grew involuntarily hard at the thought.

A coy flicker flashed in her eyes. "Your given name?"

He smirked. How odd that he'd kissed a lass who didn't even know his name.

At that moment, Thomas bellowed impatiently from the bottom of the stairs. "Tristan MacKenzie!"

Tristan exhaled and gestured toward the source of the shouting. There was her answer.

He yelled back, "Aye?"

"Marchpane!"

"On its way!"

"Tristan," Mery repeated softly. Lord, on her tongue, his name sounded like spun sugar.

Her gaze drifted down to his mouth. Before he knew what was happening, she moved toward him, catching his face between her hands. Then she pressed a light, brief kiss upon his lips.

Just as swiftly, she withdrew.

"Thank ye for the sweets...Tristan."

Then, while her kiss was still warm upon his lips, she picked up her skirts to flee down the stairs.

Tristan shook his head. Mery Graham was like a new

ingredient unexpectedly sprinkled into the recipe of his life. She was both sharp and smooth, piquant and mellow, hot and sweet. Like an unfamiliar spice, he wasn't quite sure what to do with her. But he sensed, given the opportunity to sample more of her surprising flavor, he'd figure it out soon enough.

Meanwhile, he had to finish up supper and start preparing the kitchens for the big day ahead. The prince would be baptized on the morrow. Some of the most important nobles in the world would dine in the great hall. Everything had to go smoothly. And Tristan couldn't afford to be distracted by a tempting pair of lips.

The man in the gray cloak scraped his stool closer to the peat fire of the inn at Linlithgow as he sat sipping his ale. There was something about the wretched cold in Scotland that pierced a man's hide and seeped straight into the bones. Back home in London, December brought rain and occasional snow. But it was nothing like this relentless, unforgiving, joint-throbbing chill.

Three more days. Just three more days. Then, if fortune favored him, he'd return to his beloved London.

Tomorrow morn he'd depart with the retinue of the Earl of Bedford. They'd make the formal march to Stirling for the baptism of Queen Mary's brat. After that, he'd have just three days to make his move, three days to change the fate of England.

Queen Elizabeth was unaware of the great deed he was about to perform on her behalf. She might *never* be privy to the details. If he succeeded brilliantly, she'd never suspect it was he who had saved the kingdom. If he got caught, she would of course have to publicly condemn his actions. Still, she would privately commend his sacrifice, knowing he'd done what was necessary to preserve the royal line.

All the talk of truce between Scotland and England was nonsense. The Earl of Bedford might be attending the baptism as a show of diplomacy toward Elizabeth's cousin Mary. But no one with a drop of English blood believed that Queen Mary's infant son deserved to become king. Elizabeth *would* bear a son one day, and it was *he* who would reign as the rightful heir. Mary's lad was only a pretender to the throne.

He drew the cloak tighter about him and clenched his teeth as he stared into the flames.

It irked him that Elizabeth should have to wear a mask of diplomacy. It was bad enough that she'd sent the Earl to the baptism as her ambassador of peace and good will. But to send an extravagant baptismal font as a gift to her scheming Scots cousin was an affront. The thing was enormous, made of gold and studded with precious stones. It had to have cost a fortune. It looked as if it were made for...a king.

He spat his disgust into the flames, making them sizzle.

It didn't matter. None of it mattered. Bedford would get his chance to try diplomacy. But if that didn't work, he intended to take affairs into his own hands and do what no one else was willing to do. That was the point of being a spy. Sometimes in the chess game between kingdoms, a pawn had to make sacrifices to protect his queen.

# CHAPTER 8

*DECEMBER 17*

Last night, all the way back to the minstrels' lodgings above the spectacle shop, Mery had thought about the cook's breathtaking kiss. She'd dreamt of half-naked satyrs ranging over snowbanks made of blancmange. Even this morn, climbing the hill to return to the castle, she'd been unable to think of anything but Tristan MacKenzie.

When would she see him again? How would she get him to kiss her once more? And what delectable sweet would she like to taste on his lips this time?

She was smiling in anticipation when the minstrels entered the gates of Stirling. But her smile dimmed when the minstrels were approached by a rather anxious Bastian Pagez.

"The English ambassador will not attend the baptism," he told Harry. "I can only hope the English musicians will not refuse to accompany you for the supper."

"Don't worry, sir," Harry assured him with a gracious bow. "We can perform without a consort."

"It isn't about the music," Bastian said. "It's a matter of diplomatic relations. We wish to portray the harmony of the two queens—English and Scots." He shook his head. "But how can there be harmony when Bedford is refusing to attend the ceremony?" He threw up his hands. "Please, break your fast. Certainly they will not insult the queen by refusing to attend the dinner."

Break their fast? That was fine with Mery. She couldn't wait to go to the great hall.

But to her disappointment, Tristan wasn't there. She was half tempted to creep down to the kitchens to look for him. But she couldn't afford to get into trouble today. Soon the castle would be filled with nobles. And by this evening, she'd get to sing for the new prince. This would be a once-in-a-lifetime event, and she didn't want to miss a thing.

So she hastily devoured a thick slice of barley bread with soft cheese and a cup of watered wine. Then, because she was too excited to stay indoors any longer, she slipped out to see how things were progressing.

The sun had apparently decided to keep its stubborn head beneath the covers this morn. The sky was gray and gloomy. Harry would have scolded her for wandering about the keep on such a frosty morn. He said cold air was bad for the voice.

But Mery figured she'd been breathing cold air her whole life. So far, it had done her no harm. Still, she pulled her cloak closer around her throat for good measure. Then she crossed the outer close through the crush of busy servants and headed toward the wall of the castle.

She climbed the steps up to the wall walk. From high

atop the parapets of the main gate, she had a clear view of the esplanade. What she saw made her heart flutter like the royal pennons atop the towers of Stirling.

In the distance rode hundreds of mounted knights. They paraded slowly toward the castle in a grand procession, proudly waving their banners as the townsfolk came out of their homes to greet them. Mery knew they were the nobles sent to accompany the three ambassadors—the Earl of Bedford from England, the Count of Brienne from France, and Emmanuel Philibert du Cros from Savoy.

A crush of spectators, alerted to their arrival, suddenly joined her atop the wall. Several tall men crowded in front of her, blocking her view.

Frustrated, she sought a better vantage point. The southernmost end of the wall was almost deserted. Elbowing her way through the crowd, she broke free and made her way to a low spot in the crenellated wall. From there, she found that if she gripped tightly to the stone, she could lean out over the three-story drop and, if she craned her neck, just glimpse the oncoming riders as they crested the esplanade.

It was admittedly a precarious spot, but no more dangerous than some of the trees she'd climbed in Nairn. Besides, she liked the view that being up high gave her. She felt like the queen of all she surveyed.

Standing in the gardens at the base of the castle wall, Tristan looked up and stopped dead in his tracks.

What the devil?

His heart seized. His legs turned to custard.

What was Mery Graham doing hanging over a sheer

drop like that? If she wasn't careful, she'd fall to her death.

He'd ventured to the garden to cut holly boughs to deck the roast pig platter. Now his fingers tightened on his knife as he watched the lass lean even farther over the precipice.

He wanted to bark at her to get back from the edge. But that might startle her into falling. And he didn't want to wake the queen's husband, Lord Darnley, who had refused to take part in the baptism and was probably still asleep in the chamber below.

"Psst!" he called up.

She didn't respond.

"Pssssst!"

Nothing.

"Mery!" he hissed. "Mery Graham!"

She didn't seem to hear him.

Casting about, he found the holly bushes and picked a small handful of berries. He lobbed a berry toward her. It fell short. He tried another. It landed behind her. The third one bounced off the parapet.

The fourth berry hit her head. She flinched, shaking her head and glancing up at the sky as if it had fallen from there. Then she resumed watching the procession.

He tossed another berry. It hit her on the sleeve. She frowned and flung it away.

"Mery!" he hissed again. "Me-ry!"

He dared not speak any louder, so he tried a quick volley of berries.

She batted one away, then began swatting at them so furiously, she nearly let go of the stone.

His heart lodged in his throat as she hooked her arm back around the wall before she could fall.

Then she spotted him.

"Oh. Hello!" she called down with a smile and an enthusiastic wave.

"Shh!" he warned, holding up both his hands. Unfortunately, one of them was still holding his knife.

"Zounds!" Her mouth dropped open. "What are ye doin' with that dagger?"

He grimaced, hoping Lord Darnley wasn't in earshot. Just for good measure, he put away the knife and pressed his finger to his lips. "Shh!"

She looked furtively both ways and then bent forward from the waist over the wall to hiss back, "What are ye doin', Tristan?"

"Get down from there!" he whispered furiously.

She recoiled in surprise. "Don't tell me what to do."

"Do ye want to fall and break your neck?"

"Fie! I'm not goin' to fall."

"Ye almost fell just now!"

"Don't worry about me." Then she brightened. "Hey, ye should come up. The view is amazin'. Ye can see the guests arrivin'. There's hundreds o' them."

He wished he *could* come up, mostly to haul the saucy lass away from the edge and set her back on solid ground. But he had no time. As she'd just said, there were hundreds of guests arriving. He was the man tasked with seeing them fed.

"I can't," he said. "I'm too busy."

"Wait there then," she said. "I'll come down to *ye*."

The eager light in her eyes told him that would be a mistake. She looked even more beautiful now than she had yesterday. Clad in a sumptuous gown of red brocade, she looked like a ruby set into the pale stone. One kiss, and he'd forget all about the queen's banquet.

"Nae," he told her. "I'm needed in the kitchens."

Her shoulders sank. "Ye can't spare even one moment?"

He knew better. One moment would turn into two, and then five, and then Thomas would be cursing at him for charring the roast pig.

"Sorry. What about ye?" he asked. "Aren't ye supposed to be doin' some hey-nonny-nonnies or some such?"

She giggled, and even though he feared her laughter might wake Lord Darnley, he wished she'd do it again. It was the most adorable sound.

"Aye, anon."

He shook his head, and then set about cutting the holly. By the time he headed to the kitchens, her attention was back on the arriving diplomats.

It was only as the English contingent passed through the gates that Mery realized she'd better find the rest of the minstrels. The English musicians might be arriving even now. Considering how nervous Pagez was, Harry might panic if he couldn't find her.

Rather than fight the crowd again, she decided to take the stairs alongside the palace. Somehow she got turned around in the passageways and chambers. Most of them were empty, since everyone had gone to greet the arriving guests. She exited, not into the courtyard, but onto a deserted hall.

The room was so splendid, it took her breath away. The white walls were cleverly shaded with gray to look as if they were sculpted. An enormous golden coat of arms featuring the red lion of Scotland was painted against a square blue ground above the fireplace. Highly polished tables and heavy wooden chairs with red velvet cushions furnished the chamber. But most intriguing was the ceiling.

It was subdivided into dozens of squares. Each contained an embossed roundel which featured a carved and brightly painted head. Some of the heads looked like Roman emperors, some were Scottish nobles, and some appeared to represent the Muses. She circled the room, transfixed by the faces, which seemed to gaze off into the other rooms.

Hercules battled a lion in one of them. A jester looked ready to spring from another. And staring straight down at her were the unmistakable features of Henry VIII.

Then she found herself drawn to a curious head. She moved closer to get a better look.

It was the profile of a woman with an elaborate headdress and a cherub upon her breast. But what fascinated Mery were the numbers that circled the roundel. The pattern of 1s and 0s were musical notation. She wondered what the song was.

Tilting her head, she started at what seemed to be the beginning of the piece. She hummed softly the notes of a 1 chord. Then she moved on to the 0 chord, and then back to the 1. She was about to sing the next 1 when she heard male voices coming from the adjoining chamber.

In a panic, she cast about for a place to hide. There was a large trunk set near one wall with a long velvet curtain behind it. She scrambled behind the curtain just as two men entered.

She didn't mean to listen. It was of course wrong. But it wasn't as if she could stopper her ears. Besides, their conversation was quite interesting.

"I'm sure she'll sign the treaty. Especially now."

"I'm not so certain she'll agree. She's refused in the past."

The speakers were English.

"The queen is a reasonable woman. Mary is well aware that Elizabeth has fruitful years left. She can't pretend to believe that if—God willing—Elizabeth delivers a son, he will *not* be crowned king."

"Perhaps not. But to convince her to put that into writing, especially now, when Mary has just had her *own* son..."

"You worry overmuch. Mary has agreed to meet. She's seen the generous baptism gift from Elizabeth. She can't imagine her cousin bears her any ill will."

"Even if she *does*?"

"Hist! Guard your words!"

"Trust me, Bedford. 'Twill take more than words."

Mery started. Faith, that must be the Earl of Bedford himself. But what treaty were they talking about?

"That isn't up to us. Elizabeth has made it clear. Mary cannot be allowed to groom her son for the kingship. The treaty will guarantee that."

Someone else entered the chamber—a servant by the sound of him.

"My lord, on behalf o' the queen, I regret to inform ye that Her Majesty will have to defer her meetin' with ye. The queen is indisposed at the moment with the prince, preparin' for the baptism. She hopes ye will not take offense, and she assures ye that she will make every effort to meet with ye afterward."

"I see. Give my...thanks to the queen."

The servant must have left then, for the two men began in furious whispers.

"I told you."

"Bloody hell."

"It starts with delays."

"Shite."

"Then excuses."

"I was so sure that this time—"

"What? She'd hand over the crown to her cousin?"

"We have three days here," Bedford said. "Surely she can't avoid us for three days."

The other man sighed. "I hope you're right. But I've brought along a man in case—"

"A man? What sort of man?" Bedford lowered his voice. "A spy?"

"A man willing to do what we are not," he replied, "in the unlikely event we have to resort to...unsavory means."

"Elizabeth wants that document signed at all costs," Bedford agreed.

Their words hung on the air even after they left.

At all costs? Unsavory means? What did that mean?

Mery stole from behind the curtain and carefully retraced her steps until she found herself outside again. All the way, she thought about what the Englishmen had said.

The question of the rightful heir to the throne had gone on for as long as she could remember. Both Elizabeth and Mary laid claim to the crown. But Elizabeth had no progeny. And now Mary had a son. Naturally, the English had been trying to coerce Mary to sign a document, withdrawing her right to the throne in the event Elizabeth should ever bear a child.

The English queen must have viewed the birth of Mary's son as a terrible threat. That was why she wanted the document signed at all costs.

But what were the costs? Those words, "unsavory means," sent a chill through her. If Queen Mary refused to sign, would they threaten her? Would they threaten her child?

Mery bit her lip. The baptism would begin soon. Queen Mary might be walking into a trap. She had to get word to the queen that she was in danger.

# CHAPTER 9

Tristan basted the pig as wee Easson turned it. A rib of beef was roasting on another spit. Rows of capons filled the third and fourth.

Three cooks painstakingly re-feathered geese at one table. Two more stirred the multitude of sauces simmering over the fire—gallentyne, mustard and honey, orange, wine, pepper and vinegar, ginger, sorrel. Three apprentices chopped, kneaded, peeled, and whipped various ingredients that would be required for the baptismal supper.

But even though Tristan's mind was juggling a hundred things, it kept drifting back to Mery Graham.

He wondered if he'd get a chance to hear her sing at supper. He imagined she would sound like an angel, her sweet voice echoing in the great hall as she sang praises to the prince.

"Tristan!"

He almost spilled a ladle full of drippings onto the turnbrochie at the sound of her voice. What the devil?

"Tristan! Are ye there?"

Breathless, beautiful, and distraught, Mery rushed through the smoky doorway. "Thank God ye're here."

He wanted to be vexed. He'd banished her from the kitchens. But it was so hard to be angry with her when she was such a welcome feast for the eyes.

Still, he knew others were watching. So he wiped his hands on a rag, slapped it over his shoulder, and sternly approached her.

"Mery Graham, what are ye doin' down here? I told ye—"

She waved away his concerns. "Never mind that. I've got somethin' of utmost importance to tell ye."

He waited. When she didn't continue, he lifted a brow in question.

"Well, not here," she said, "not in front of everyone."

He truly did not have time for this. But he couldn't resist those beautiful hazel eyes. "Where then?"

She frowned, then brightened. "The confectionary?"

Not in a thousand years, he thought. His body, however, had other ideas. It perked up at the notion.

"The master cook is in there," he told her, fairly sure that wasn't at all true.

She looked distraught, eyeing the corners of the kitchens for a place they could speak in private.

"Why don't ye just whisper?" he suggested.

Even as he said the words, he realized that was a bad idea. Hearing her soft words, feeling her warm breath against his ear, her lips close enough to kiss...

She tugged at his shirt, pulling him forward so she could reach his ear to whisper, "The queen is in danger."

He blinked. That wasn't quite the message he was expecting. "What?"

"I said, the queen is in danger."

"Danger? What kind o' danger?" Bloody hell. Had she choked on his fallow deer pasty? Had the pickled eel disagreed with her?

She leaned toward him again. "I o'erheard the Earl o' Bedford sayin' he was goin' to force the queen to sign a paper."

"What?"

"I said, I o'erheard the Earl o'—"

"Aye, I heard ye. But what do ye mean?" To be honest, he was just relieved the queen hadn't fallen sick on his food. "What paper?"

"A paper to make sure Mary's son will ne'er be crowned king."

He smirked. "Well, she won't sign that."

"Aye, 'tis what I fear."

He frowned.

She continued. "Ye see, if she refuses, the Earl has vowed to use...'unsavory means' to convince her to sign it."

Tristan wondered why a minstrel would be concerned with the politics of the royals. Indeed, he wondered if Mery had even heard what she *thought* she'd heard. Maybe she liked to stir up mischief where there was none. Furthermore, he didn't quite know what she expected him to do about it.

Still, he supposed he was flattered that she'd come to him for help. She must believe he had some standing with the queen. He didn't want to disappoint her.

He scratched thoughtfully at his chin. "'Tis a rather vague threat. I wouldn't worry too much about it. We're in Scotland, after all. And the queen has guards protectin' her...unless..."

"Aye?"

"'*Unsavory* means.'" His lip twitched. "Ye don't think he means to add pepper to the cherry tarts?"

She gasped and shoved at his shoulder. "'Tisn't a laughin' matter, MacKenzie."

He couldn't help but grin. She was beautiful, even when she was peeved at him.

She planted her fists on her hips and forgot to whisper. "I'm speakin' about the safety o' the bloody queen, ye big oaf."

The entire staff went quiet.

Tristan grimaced, instantly remembering why it was a bad idea to have a woman in the kitchens.

"Back to work!" he shouted at them.

They snapped to. But Mery still had a look of challenge on her face. "So?"

"So?"

"What are we goin' to do about it?"

"What exactly do ye think a cook and a minstrel can do about it?"

She furrowed her brows. "I dinna ken. But we've got to keep the bairn safe."

"The bairn?"

"The prince."

Tristan thought the prince was probably the most protected bairn in all of history. The wee child had four ladies to rock him, two to dress him, three gentlemen to watch over him, four nurses, and even a man to monitor his intake of ale.

Mery may indeed have heard some nasty English remark. There had always been disagreements over which queen's son should reign. But this baptism was to be a peaceable event.

"So," she asked again, "what do ye think we should do?"

He tried to think of words to satisfy her. "What *can* we do? Watch and wait. Keep our eyes open and our ears alert."

She nodded.

He added, "But I wouldn't fret o'ermuch. 'Twould be foolhardy to threaten the queen in her own keep. Bedford isn't even attendin' the baptism, from what I hear. None o' the Protestants are. And as for the supper, the theme is reconciliation."

He knew he shouldn't take the time to explain. He had sauces to finish and custards to start. But he had an irresistible urge to put a smile back on Mery's face.

"'Tis quite clever of Bastian Pagez," he confided. "The Protestant Bedford and the Catholic Seton will be carryin' white staffs as a sign o' peace. Then at supper, the Catholics will be servin' the Protestants, and the Protestants will be servin' the Catholics."

She shrugged, only half convinced. She lowered her eyes and ran a finger along the edge of the table. "Bedford sounded rather determined."

"Well, don't let it worry ye. All that frettin' will make sour notes in your singin'." He dragged the rag from off his shoulder. "Are ye goin' to be doin' your fa-la-las today?"

"Aye, in a bit." She nodded to the men re-feathering the geese. "What are they doin' there?"

Glad for the change of subject, he followed her glance. "Them? They're dressin' the roast swans. Ye see, they take all the feathers and..."

When he turned back, her mouth was full of food and her eyes were full of guilt.

"Did ye just steal a pasty?" he asked.

She shook her head.

He gave the little liar a sly smile. "How is it?"

"Mmf, good, mm-hm."

He should scold her, but he didn't have the heart. How could he scold a lass who loved his cooking?

"MacKenzie!" came a familiar bellow, definitely *not* from the confectionary.

"Shite," Tristan hissed.

For just an instant, he considered stashing the lass under the table where the master cook wouldn't see her.

But Mery had already thought of a plan. Seizing him by the front of his shirt, she hauled him forward and kissed him.

Her mouth was soft and warm on his. When she wrapped her arms possessively around his neck, it was only natural to pull her closer. And she was right. The spicy sauce from the pasty on her lips had just the right amount of pepper.

The sudden bang of the master cook's palm on the table broke them apart.

Thomas glared at Mery and pointed a finger toward the door. "Out!"

# CHAPTER 10

From what the man had determined in his first few hours at Stirling Castle, Queen Mary's whelp was under constant supervision. At any given time, half a dozen servants cooed over the child, seeing to his every need, from combing his hair to wiping his arse.

There had to be some way to penetrate that wall of protection, whether by stealth or wiles. All he required was a moment's access.

The babe was such a small thing, not even capable of walking. It would be child's play to smother it, twist its tiny neck, or drop it from the parapets.

Indeed, it occurred to him with grim humor that the extravagant baptismal font Queen Elizabeth had sent was large enough to drown a small child. He smirked, wondering if that was unintentional.

Unfortunately, Bedford and the entire Protestant contingent had refused to attend the Catholic baptism, or else he might have had his chance to do just that.

Still, he could hear the monks in the chapel, singing holy and obsequious praises to the new prince. It was sickening, the way the Scots doted on the child and the way the English pretended his birth was somehow significant.

Bedford had failed to secure Mary's signature on the treaty. She'd refused to even give the earl an audience. No doubt she would continue to do so, no matter how positive Bedford was that the Scottish queen would see reason.

Reason? Preposterous! How could reason compete with maternal instincts? She would keep putting Bedford off with excuse after excuse until the English were forced to harsher measures.

But why wait? With one swift and violent act, *he* could solve everything. And so he'd continue to look for an opportunity. When the right moment arose, he would be prepared.

Mery wished she could watch the baptism. Only the most elite of the nobles were invited. Since the ceremony was held in the chapel, it was monks and not minstrels who sang the sacred music. She took heart in the fact that the English weren't in attendance either. At least for the next few hours, they could do the queen and her bairn no harm.

Immediately after the baptism, Harry called for the minstrels to meet with the consort of English musicians for a quick rehearsal before supper. Though the English diplomat might be a threat, Mery wasn't too concerned about the English musicians.

Musicians crossed borders all the time. They seldom had strong allegiances to any country. They were always the best ambassadors, since they spoke the common language of song. Indeed, it had been Pagez's intent to use the natural diplomacy between musicians to play upon the theme of reconciliation.

The five men of the English consort proved to be entertaining characters. The hurdy-gurdy player was as old and cranky as his instrument. The harpist was full of sarcasm and biting wit. The lutist spoke as softly as his lute. The viol player was moody and melancholy. And the tambor player was a lad who lisped and giggled like a lass.

They proved to be competent players, for which Mery was thankful. As Tristan had agreed, she needed to have her eyes and ears free to watch for suspicious activity.

It was almost evening when, with a fanfare of trumpets, supper was announced in the great hall.

The minstrels and consort performed *Tant que vivray* as the guests entered. When Mery glimpsed the stunning and stately Queen Mary holding the ermine-robed prince in her arms, her heart skipped a beat. Thankfully, she didn't miss a beat of the music.

Mery's eyes welled with tears of devotion as she sang from her heart: *Toute ma vie, je l'aymeray et chanteray, c'est la premiere, c'est la derniere que j'ay servie et serviray, All my life, I will love her and sing of her, she is the first, she is the last that I have served and will serve.*

But when the Earl of Bedford was announced, she almost choked on her lyrics. He looked so much more imposing and dangerous than he had sounded. While he might be carrying a white staff of truce, Mery imagined that staff could also be used as a weapon.

After the introductory song, the minstrels retired to a small chamber off one end of the great hall, where costumed actors prepared for the court masque to follow the meal. The area was separated by a curtain so that

Pagez, directing the festivities, could discreetly watch the progress of the supper and send the minstrels out as needed. The musicians took advantage of the curtain as well, taking turns to peer out at the noble guests between performing.

Despite wishing to impress the queen and maintain an air of decorum, Mery nearly burst into laughter as the re-feathered birds were served to the strains of *Il bianco e dolce cigno, The white and gentle swan,* which compared the sad death song of the swan to the joyful "little death" of lovemaking.

Once safely behind the curtain again, Mery watched as course after course was served. Her stomach grumbled. She hoped Tristan would save some of that roast pig for the minstrels, as well as a bite of goose, a pasty, a bit of venison, and whatever was in that beautiful gold custard dish.

Beside her, the hurdy-gurdy player groused, "You watch. They won't have any bustard left for the likes of us."

"Bustard?" Mery had never eaten bustard, which was a large bird. Maybe it tasted like heron.

The harpist chimed in, "'Tis his favorite. Or so he says. I don't think he's ever eaten it."

The hurdy-gurdy player frowned. "I figure it must be good, because they never have any left."

Even the grim violist laughed at that.

Mery straightened with pride. "I know the cook. Perhaps I can get ye a bit o' bustard."

The lute player sighed. "Everything looks so delicious."

Mery smiled in agreement. "Doesn't it?"

"Oh, aye," the tambor player said with lascivious languor. "*Most* delicious. Savory. Tempting. Irresistible."

Mery followed his gaze.

He was staring at Tristan MacKenzie.

She'd never heard a man extol the virtues of another man quite so boldly, though she knew musicians who had similar appetites. Still, once she laid eyes on Tristan, she had to agree with the tambor player.

Tristan looked splendid. No longer in his stained shirt and rumpled trews, he wore a modest doublet of dark blue, trimmed tastefully with black cord, black breeches, a flat black cap to match, and tall black boots. His face was clean, and his hair was combed. Indeed, he looked so refined, standing there with his hands clasped behind his back, overseeing the service, that Mery could have easily mistaken him for a noble.

"You can have your bustard," the tambor player said, smacking his lips. "I'll have a bite of *that.*"

Inexplicably, Mery's hackles rose as she declared, "'Tisn't yours for the havin', tambor man."

The other musicians chortled at her vehement words. She blushed. What caused her to suddenly feel so possessive about Tristan, she didn't know. After all, he didn't belong to her. In three days, she'd be gone and might never see him again.

Still, she believed in seizing the day. And she wasn't about to let a mincing English fop get in her way.

# CHAPTER 11

So far, Tristan thought the dinner was going well. Nothing was burnt. No one was sick. The courses were arriving on time.

He was far from comfortable, however, trapped in the confines of a tightly buttoned doublet with his legs stuffed into thigh-high boots. He'd prefer to remain below in his shirt and trews. But Thomas had needed someone he could rely on to supervise the service in the great hall. Naturally, he called on his right-hand man.

Tristan pretended he was at ease, clasping his hands behind his back, when in truth he was only stifling his fidgety fingers. He felt...useless.

Of course, his presence was anything but useless. It was up to him to ensure that the ambassadors liked their food. It was a delicate situation, pleasing diplomats from four different countries. The dishes had been carefully selected to include nods to each of their cultures. But of course, mistakes were possible.

History was in the making. And slights were unforgivable.

It was another reason he preferred cooking for ordinary folk. With ordinary folk, he wasn't on trial for his cooking every time he served supper. His reputation didn't rest on creating flawless dishes for every meal. He could experiment, play, and, aye, ruin a dish now and then without risking his position.

He preferred cooking for simple folk like Mery. His lips curved into a smile at the memory of her stealing that pasty. He liked people who visibly appreciated his cooking—licking their fingers, making appetizing murmurs, and closing their eyes in pleasure.

While the nobles might be pleased, they seldom raved over a meal. After all, that might be perceived as an admission that one's own cook was not as skilled as that of the host. But he knew they always mentally catalogued the dishes they liked and tried to have their own cooks imitate them. He didn't doubt that, after tonight, they'd all try to recreate his incomparable rib of beef with pepper and vinegar sauce.

Finally the third course was cleared away. He was free to go back to the kitchens. But he knew Mery would be singing again soon for the masque. So he decided to linger above stairs for a moment.

The songs were in Italian, but the masque wasn't too difficult to decipher. The presentation seemed to center around good will and peace between the countries.

Mery's voice blended in seamlessly with those of the other singers and the musicians. But the glow of delight in her face was all her own.

More than once, she caught his eye. In that instant, he felt as if she sang to him alone. That look made his heart leap.

A few times, the man playing the tambor also gave him a look—a strange, languid look. In fact, he stared at Tristan with such intimate intensity, Tristan began to wonder if perhaps the man was acquainted with him.

Partway through the entertainment, the infant prince—apparently not caring for the music and beginning to fuss—was whisked away by four of his guardians.

By the time the men in horse costumes came out for the final *ballet de cour*, everyone was deep in their cups and caught up in the gaiety. Even the stuffy Earl of Bedford, whose religion frowned on dancing, allowed his men to join in the merrymaking.

Before Tristan knew what was happening, Mery rushed up beside him in a whirl of ruby skirts and grabbed his hand.

"*O occhi manza mia,*" she sang with the others as she pulled him toward the middle of the great hall and into the dancing fray.

He stiffened. He didn't know how to dance, not properly. But he couldn't exactly refuse. With the queen watching, he didn't dare engage in a battle of wills with the lass.

"*O occhi manza mia,*"she sang again, her eyes sparkling, "*cigli dorati!*"

He had no idea what she was singing about, but he didn't care. Her gaze was filled with flirtation. That was enough for him.

"I don't know how to dance," he blurted out between her lines of song.

She just grinned and tugged him along. He tried as best he could to imitate the dancers around him, who twirled and turned and bowed with easy grace.

*"O faccia d'una luna stralucente!"* she sang, enchanting him with the beatific expression on her face.

He couldn't help but smile. For all he knew, she was telling him he had the face of a frog and the breath of a pig. But the coy adoration in her eyes dazzled him. He'd never seen a woman so full of life and fun.

At last she slowed and sang the final phrase, *"Fa mi contento."*

She gave him a charming curtsey, and he bowed. The guests cheered and applauded, and she winked at him.

"Ye dance very well for a satyr," she teased.

He shook his head. He still didn't know what a satyr was. "Ye sing pretty well for a mere mortal."

"But I'm not fishworthy?" She raised a brow.

It took him a moment to remember. He would have apologized finally then for ever having said her angelic voice scared fish. But the consort started another tune.

*"O Lucia"!* 'Tis one o' my favorites," Mery said, clapping her hands.

"Oh, lass, I wish I could dance with ye all night. Truly I do. But I can't," he told her with a bereaved smile. "When ye're a cook, there's always the next meal to prepare."

She gave him a nod of understanding.

"I'll see ye later then," she promised.

And then she was off and singing a merry tune, weaving through the hobbyhorses like an enchanting sprite.

It turned out the hurdy-gurdy player was right. They didn't get any bustard for supper. They didn't get much of anything. The greedy nobles had gobbled it all up. The musicians were forced to make do with venison pottage and bread, with a wee bit of applemoise and mugs of beer.

Mery was disappointed, even more so that Tristan was nowhere to be found. After boasting that she knew the cook, the English consort only gave her pitying smiles as they supped on the meager fare.

Mery poked at her pottage. To be truthful, it wasn't meager. It was the finest venison pottage she'd ever eaten. And most of the time at these events, she wasn't given a sweet afterward. The applemoise was lovely, sprinkled with cinnamon and sugar.

It was just that, after watching the nobles dine on such exotic fare, her appetite had been whetted for so much more. Singing and dancing always made her incredibly hungry. And she'd really wanted to try that roast pork.

It was growing late. Some of the servants had already begun to bed down in the great hall. But Harry had imbibed heavily. She knew it would be hours before he collected the minstrels to return to their lodgings, if he didn't pass out first. There was time to steal into the kitchens and look for something more substantial to eat.

Slipping away from the table, she made her way out, over the bridge, and along the darkened passage to the kitchens.

They appeared to be deserted. The fires were banked. The spits were empty. The cooks were gone.

Tucking her lip beneath her teeth, she squinted into the dim chamber, searching the table tops for any food that might be left.

Tristan raised the candle to the shelf of spices so he could see the rows of clay pots and vials. He set the grains of Paradise next to the ginger.

He'd sent the staff to bed. The morn would start early enough. The courses Thomas Chalmers and he had sketched out for the morrow were even more challenging than today's. To make matters worse, because Pagez was partial to drama and whimsy, the servers would be wearing costumes. He hoped none of his lads would be adorned with feathers, for if they strayed too near the fire, they'd be turned into phoenixes.

In any case, he wanted the staff well-rested and alert. So he'd told the master cook he'd empty the kitchens and bank the fires for the night. Tristan himself planned to retire after he locked up the precious spices.

When he heard a noise coming from the stairs, he turned with a suspicious scowl.

It wasn't the staff. The staff wouldn't be so stealthy.

For a brief instant, he thought of the murderous English traitor Mery believed was skulking about, then dismissed the idea.

Still, he extinguished the candle between his thumb and finger.

Even if the intruder was only a common thief, the spices were a valuable commodity. That was why they were kept under lock and key. Tristan wasn't about to let a mischief-maker rob him of his saffron.

Unfortunately, the spicery contained no weapons—no knives, no pokers, not even a heavy iron pan. About the best he could do against a thief was to use his apron and the element of surprise.

He held his breath as he heard the cautious footfalls coming closer. When he sensed the intruder was no less than a foot away, he whipped his apron out and brought it down over the villain's head, trapping him in a web of grease-spattered linen.

While the hooded thief was flustered and flailing about, Tristan seized him by the shoulders and shoved him up against the plaster wall.

"A-ha!" he cried in triumph.

The reply was difficult to make out with the muffling cloth, but it sounded like a curse. And it was definitely not the voice of a thieving knave.

He grimaced at his mistake, immediately releasing his prisoner. Of *course*. It was the mischievous Mery Graham. He carefully removed the apron from her head.

"Sorry, las—"

The punch hit him square on the nose and rocked his head back. Stars exploded in his vision an instant before he felt the eye-watering pain. He staggered back a step, then bent forward with a groan to cradle his injured nose in his hands.

# CHAPTER 12

"Tristan?" She seemed surprised.

"Why did ye do that?" he moaned.

"Ye frightened me."

"Ye hit me."

"Well...ye deserved it."

How could Tristan argue with that? He *had* pushed her up against the wall.

Still covering his nose with one hand, he dabbed underneath it with the apron, concerned that it might be bleeding. He sucked a painful breath through his teeth.

"What are ye doin', sneakin' around my kitchens anyway?"

"I'm half-starved."

"What?" For a cook, her words carried more impact than her punch. "Were ye not fed?"

"A wee bit o' venison pottage. Some bread. Applemoise. And beer," she admitted.

Faith! What more did the wee lass want? That was more than he'd eaten himself.

"But we got no roast pig," she said on a pout. "And no bustard."

87

"Bustard?"

"Aye," she said with an injured sniff. "I was lookin' forward to the bustard. We *all* were."

He furrowed his brows. "I didn't serve any bustard."

"Oh."

He shook his head. He couldn't guess what they'd imagined was bustard. "Ye know, I've had harsh critics of my cookin' before," he complained, "but none o' them ever clouted me."

"Sorry."

"For a lass, ye throw a mean punch."

She clucked her tongue and pulled his hand down from his face. "Here, ye big bairn. Let's go where there's light, and I'll take a look at that."

"Fine," he said, following her carefully down the stairs toward the main kitchens, where they could see by the glowing coals. "And I'm *not* a big bairn."

"Ach! I didn't even come close to breakin' your nose."

His nose didn't seem to be bleeding, but it still hurt like hell. "By heaven, lass, are ye in the *habit* o' breakin' people's noses?"

She shrugged. "I have five brothers."

He arched a brow. "Ah, the Cruiknose clan."

She giggled. It was an adorable sound. If his face hadn't been throbbing, he might have joined in.

She caught his chin carefully between her fingers and examined his face, turning his head this way and that. Lord, she looked beautiful in the low firelight. It was hard to imagine that, a few moments ago, her delicate hand had cracked his nose.

"I think ye'll live," she proclaimed. "Beside, ye look more distinguished with that bit of a twist in your nose."

He caught her fingers in his. "Ye're a wicked minx. Did ye know that?"

"Oh, aye." She grinned.

He resisted the urge to kiss her fingertips. He really didn't have time for this. He released her hand.

She walked her fingers up the middle of his chest. "So have ye got a slice o' that fine roast pork for a poor, starvin' minstrel lass?"

He wished he had a whole hock for her. Sadly, the nobles had made quick work of it. "Alas, 'tis all gone."

Her face fell. But even if she hadn't given him that pitiful look, he would have found something for her to eat. He was a cook. It was against his nature to let a soul go hungry.

"If ye'll put away that pout," he said, "I'll cook ye up some eggs."

"Eggs?"

"Ye *do* like eggs?"

She shrugged.

"Ye'll love these eggs," he promised.

He stirred the coals of one of the ovens to life and set a small iron skillet atop the flame. Then he tied on his apron, giving her a wink as she stood with her hands clasped beneath her chin, watching in fascination.

He scooped a generous portion of butter into the pan. When it began to bubble, he snatched an egg from the basket. Showing off a bit, with one hand, he cracked it on the edge of the skillet, dropped the contents into the pan, then discarded the shell.

"More?" he asked.

She nodded. He added another.

"Mm, one more," she told him.

He added a third. While they softly sizzled, he added a

pinch of salt and a dash of pepper. He picked up the pan and swirled it gently around, making sure to leave the yolks intact.

He hadn't realized until that moment how much he missed cooking. It seemed he was so busy supervising the other staff that he had little time to get his own hands into the pots and pans. In fact, it was so enjoyable to cook for the lass, who watched him with bated breath, that he decided to show her a few of his special skills.

When the eggs were fairly firm on the underside, he picked up the pan and slid it in a circular motion to loosen the eggs. Then, with a flick of his wrist, he turned the eggs over in midair, catching them carefully again in the pan before he set it back down on the fire.

She clapped with glee.

From the board full of condiments, he flipped the bottle to add a splash of verjuice, then dumped a dollop of mustard sauce to the pan, whisking it over the top of the eggs. Turning his back, he sprinkled crystals of salt over his shoulder into the pan with perfect aim. When the whites of the eggs were set, he slid the dish onto a wooden platter and added a crust of leftover pandemain.

He offered it to her with a regal flourish. "My lady."

Her eyes twinkled. "How do you eat it?"

He dipped the crust into the eggs, coating the bread with a good portion of golden yolk and the mustard sauce. Then he lifted it to her mouth.

She took a quick bite before it could drip. In the process, she grazed his fingertip with her lips. A warm shiver pulsed through him.

"Mmmm." Her eyes closed in delight as she slowly chewed and swallowed, then licked her lips.

He felt his blood begin to simmer as his gaze was drawn to her delicious mouth.

He wanted to kiss her.

Instead, he fed her another bite.

She slurped it up with a soft moan of pleasure.

Beneath his apron, desire was making its presence known. He tried to ignore it.

She dipped two fingers into the middle of the eggs, coating them with the warm, molten yolk. Then she brushed the mixture over his lips and, before he could open his mouth to tell her nae, she leaned forward and stole a kiss.

It was then he realized it was pointless to resist.

# CHAPTER 13

ow Tristan had made such simple ingredients so delicious, Mery didn't know. But they tasted even more amazing from his mouth. She licked the tangy mixture from his lips, then slipped her tongue past them in a savory trespass.

He groaned lightly, which made her heart flutter in excitement. When she would have delved farther into his mouth, he pushed her away, but only so he could return the favor. Her heart raced as he dipped a finger into the yolk and swept it across her mouth.

He followed up by lapping softly at her lips, leaving her gasping with need.

They continued feeding each other, one delicious bite at a time, until the platter of eggs was gone. Then, though one hunger had been satisfied, another was only stirring. Inspired, Mery glanced at the row of condiments on the board. "Is that honey?"

He nodded.

She reached over and slid the pot toward her.

"What are ye doin', lass?" he whispered.

"Havin' a sweet to balance the savory," she purred.

Opening the lid, she stuck her finger into the sticky liquid and sampled it, licking the sweet stuff from the tip of her finger.

"Oh, lass," he breathed.

She took his hand then and dipped his forefinger deep into the pot, coating it with honey. But instead of giving him a taste, she gave him a coy grin and brought it to her own mouth. She wrapped her lips around his finger and sucked every bit of the sweet syrup from it.

He made a sound as if he were strangling then. His face grew deadly serious. His jaw clenched. His eyes glowed like smoldering coals. For an instant, she thought he was angry with her for stealing the honey.

But then he pressed forward, engaging her fully, angling his head to cover her mouth with his own in a greedy kiss.

The first time he'd kissed her, Mery had been caught off guard. Surprise had made the unexpected kiss exciting.

But this... This was altogether different.

There was so much passion and craving in this kiss. He devoured her as if he were starving and she were the most delectable, irresistible dish he'd ever consumed.

Her heart throbbed. Warm blood sang in her veins. Her hands found their way into his hair, tangling there and drawing him closer.

His kisses became more frantic, more ravenous. She should have been frightened. But she felt exhilarated. With naked desire, she pressed her bosom against his chest and opened her mouth to him. At her invitation, he thrust his tongue boldly into her mouth. Beneath the apron, she felt him grow hard and eager.

The empty platter clattered to the floor as he freed his

hands to clasp her closer. He growled against her mouth. She gasped at the dizzying dilemma—being trapped in his embrace, yet feeling no desire to leave it.

As if the kitchens were aflame, she felt searing heat scorch her skin. Breathless with hunger and incapable of speech, she moaned her nameless need against his cheek.

His hand strayed then, grazing her bare shoulder. With the back of his knuckles, he caressed the sensitive skin of her bosom. And then he dipped his fingers lower, sliding them gently under the neckline of her linen underdress, teasing at the crease between her breasts.

She sighed in wonder at the lovely sensation. Wanting more, she loosened the ties of her stiff stomacher.

Encouraged by her invitation, he slowly slipped his callused fingers farther inside to cup her breast.

How delightfully forbidden it felt to be touched there. When he weighed her in his palm, she smiled in pleasure.

But when his thumb brushed over her nipple, her smile became a gasp of utter astonishment. His caress created a heavenly friction that seemed to set every nerve on fire. She pressed her hips against his, wanting even more of him.

"Oh, lass," he sighed against her mouth. "Maybe we shouldn't."

Mery was having none of that. "Oh, aye, we should."

"The others..."

"Fie on the others."

"Harry?" he gasped out.

"Drinkin'."

He hesitated only a moment. Then he hauled back her stomacher and lowered his head, enclosing her breast in his warm, wet mouth.

She arched her neck back. A divine current hummed through her entire body. She felt illuminated, alight with awe.

He lapped at her until she was as stiff as the peak of the meringues. Then he moved to her other breast.

She sobbed with joy. A haze of desire softened everything around her, even as her nipple hardened.

Still she hungered. A sharp craving centered between her legs, and she longed to have him touch her there.

At last he released her breast and came back to her mouth, kissing her with a tenderness that intensified the ache beneath her skirts.

Never had she felt such powerful yearning. She suddenly wanted to taste him in the same way. She untied her cap and flung it off. Then she raked back his shirt and kissed her way down his chest.

He chuckled softly as she nuzzled the linen aside and finally found his flat nipple.

She sucked his flesh gently between her lips, and then made her way to the other side, leaving a trail of wet kisses.

His chest swelled with a deep breath as he hung his head atop hers.

When she returned to his mouth again, she could taste the desperation there.

"Ah, lass," he gasped out between kisses, "ye play...a dangerous game."

Nothing could incite her more. "Do I?" she asked coyly.

"Are ye sure ye..."

"What?" she teased. "Want this?" She ran the tip of her tongue across his lips.

He made a sound that was half-laugh, half-moan.

The current between her legs was not abating.

"Oh, aye, I want ye," she told him.

Then, with brazen yearning, she reached between them and pressed her palm against his firm staff. He sucked in a sharp breath, which only increased her desire. She rubbed across him, massaging him through his apron and breeches.

"Do ye want *me?*" she whispered.

His answer was a groaning chuckle.

She reached behind him and tugged loose the strings of his apron, letting it fall to the floor.

"Oh, lass," he wheezed, "do ye know what ye're doin' to me?"

"Oh, aye," she lied. She had no idea what she was doing to him. But that had never stopped her before. "Do ye?"

He laughed. "Aye."

Then a terrible thought occurred to her. "Ye aren't...married...are ye?"

He smiled. "Only to my work. And ye?"

She shook her head.

This was perfect, she thought. Long ago, she'd learned to live for the moment, to take advantage of opportunity when it presented itself, to strike while the iron was hot. Swiving was something she'd never tried. And she couldn't think of someone with whom she'd rather try it.

Tristan had never swived a woman in the kitchens. He'd trysted in plenty of other places. In the stables. Behind the henhouse. Under the Stirling Bridge. Even in his own bed on occasion. But it seemed wicked to do such a thing in the place where he worked every day...which made it all the more exciting.

Mery Graham made the kitchens seem like a sensuous paradise. Untroubled by the smoke or the smells, she behaved as if she cared about nothing but him. So when he lifted her up to sit on the edge of the table beside the basket of eggs, the pot of butter, and sacks of onions to hike up her skirts, she made no protest. A lass like Mery, always on the road, had probably learned to take pleasure in whatever coupling corners she found.

She helped him unlace his breeches, scrabbling with eager fingers.

When he wrenched down his trews and freed his staff, she gave a small gasp of awe. For one instant, he worried that perhaps she might not be as experienced as she said.

But when she reached out to stroke him—her touch like velvet upon his sensitive skin—his fears vanished.

When he dipped his fingers into the butter, slathering himself with it, her eyes glimmered in fascination. He felt no hesitation at all when he eased forward, sheathing himself in her welcoming warmth.

She whistled in a quick breath, and her fingers tightened on his shoulders. He wondered if something was wrong, if he'd hurt her somehow. He searched her eyes. But they were shadowed. And when she opened them again, she gave him a quivering smile.

For an extended moment he simply rested inside her. Closing his eyes, relishing the blissful sensation of all that womanly flesh surrounding him, he tipped his brow onto the top of her head.

And then he began the slippery seduction that would blend their bodies into one delicious and perfect dish.

He pulled her hips close to his, coaxing her to wrap her legs about his waist.

She responded, pressing closer and nestling her forehead in the crook of his neck. Her tresses felt like silk where they lashed his skin. Gradually, she began rubbing against him in a seductive effort to relieve the lustful itch between her thighs. Soon he felt her hot, uneven breath across his throat.

It took all his willpower to maintain control. Lovemaking was a delicate process. A lass was like a bowl of fresh cream, fragile and sweet. While Tristan might command her with constant and uncompromising plunges, he had to guard against too much force. Though he pounded into her with steady repetition, he took special care to retain his tenderness.

Her skin grew slick with sweat as she dug her heels into his buttocks. He supported the weight of her small breasts as he kissed the soft shell of her ear. The more violent his thrusts became, the lighter were his caresses.

Her fingers began to squeeze his shoulders with increasing tension. Suddenly, a look of unfocused wonder came over her beatific face. Her mouth dropped open. She froze for one ecstatic moment, catching her breath over and over.

When her passion finally burst into a series of satiated spasms, it was with a low cry that sent him over the edge.

He pulled out of her then for safety's sake. But desire pumped from him, flowing like honey from a crushed comb. Such strong shudders rocked him that he was amazed he could still stand. Their gasps intertwined in the firelight.

Once he'd caught his breath, he whispered, "Are ye all right?"

"Aye," she breathed. "Oh, aye. Most definitely aye."

He grinned. Nothing could have pleased him more. In the aftermath of their passion, he held her close, stroking her glossy hair, feeling her tremble. He'd never felt so well-matched or engaged by a woman before.

He wanted to hold her in his arms forever.

That thought shocked the hell out of him. Aye, she was delicious, like a rare and special course served once in a lifetime. But that was all.

The spirited lass was a minstrel. She traveled the world, flitting from man to man. She was used to sharing her charms while guarding her heart.

So was he.

So why did this feel different?

Thomas was right. Tristan had an important occupation. He should treat Mery as a tasty diversion, no more.

And yet he couldn't help but feel that the lass was more than that. She was a full-course meal unto herself, with a sweet at the end. To his amazement, Tristan thought he could subsist quite nicely on a steady diet of Mery Graham.

Of course it was not to be. The bittersweet reality was that she didn't feel the same way about him.

She had her singing.

He had his cooking.

People like them had to take pleasure in the wee perfect moments where they could.

So he sighed and nestled closer to her, thinking nothing could ruin *this* perfect moment.

Then he heard her sniffling.

His heart sank. Pretending not to notice, he silently smoothed down her skirts and tied up his breeches.

No matter what she'd claimed, obviously she was *not* all

right. He didn't know what that sniffling meant, but it couldn't be good.

Mery didn't know why she was weeping.

Aye, she'd just lost her virginity. But it had to happen sometime. And it didn't even mean that much to her.

Swiving had been just one of those challenges she'd always intended to indulge in one day. Tristan had seemed like a good man for the task. And now had seemed like a good time. She'd assumed she'd do the deed, congratulate herself on her endeavor, and tick it off of her list of life accomplishments.

Never had she imagined it would have such a soul-searing impact on her.

Making love was not a light undertaking after all. It was like singing the most amazing madrigal—one written by God himself.

The counterpoint was exquisite. The harmonies were heavenly. At the very climax of the piece, when the musical tension was at its highest, the two of them had sung together in pure and perfect unison.

And just like a brilliant and moving piece of music, the performance had brought her to tears.

It was completely unexpected and mystifying.

It was also deeply troubling.

Mery had been transformed by what they'd shared. She felt connected to him now. Now she longed to remain with him...forever.

That realization was a shock. Restless Mery, who couldn't wait to leave behind her suitors in Nairn, wanted to tie her fortunes to a stranger in Stirling.

Of course that could never be. Tristan might not even care for her. Indeed, she was sure that, for a man that handsome, coupling was a frequent pastime.

Besides, even if he did care for her, their lives were too different. He had to remain at Stirling. She had to travel with the minstrels. In three days, they would part ways and probably never meet again.

The thought made her eyes well with tears once more.

She blinked them back and flashed him a tight smile, hiding her sorrow the same way she'd hidden her pain a moment ago.

It was no use letting him know her heart was aching. She might feel a powerful bond to him. But he couldn't feel the same way. He probably swived lasses all the time. He couldn't form attachments with all of them.

She was about to make some flippant reassuring remark when there was a sound in the passageway.

Thinking fast, she hopped down from the table. Crouched low in hiding, she repaired her garments.

Tristan tugged his shirt back over his shoulders and called out to the intruder. "Pattie! Ye're up early."

"Got to get a start on the pandemain," the man replied.

"Let me help ye with that," Tristan said, ushering the baker toward the bakehouse.

Mery bit her lip. If the baker was already up and about, the others would be coming soon. Quickly, before the master chef could find her, she exited the kitchens and went to find Harry. With any luck, he'd be sober enough to walk back to their lodgings.

# CHAPTER 14



"**Y**our eyes are red," Thomas observed, lifting a spoon full of boiled mutton with capers for Tristan to taste.

"'Tis only the smoke," Tristan lied. He took the bite, smacking his lips. "Maybe a bit o' lemon?"

Thomas nodded. "Wat!" he called across the kitchens. "Fetch me three lemons!"

Tristan rubbed his gritty eyes. He was exhausted. It wasn't only that he'd stayed up most of the night. What little sleep he'd managed to get, dozing in his chambers above the kitchens, was riddled with nightmares—nightmares about losing Mery Graham.

Which was ridiculous. He didn't *own* Mery Graham in the first place.

Yet somehow, after last night, he felt as if she belonged to him, as if they belonged together.

It was a pointless fantasy, he thought as he stirred oats

into the leek and turnip pottage. In the feast of Mery's life, he was but one course. Soon she'd be dining on others, leaving a trail of crumbs all across Scotland. He should be content that she'd decided to taste his wares at all.

Besides, his dedication and the nature of his work meant a life spent in the kitchens. He had no right to lay claim to such a fine lass while he toiled night and day in smoke and sweat.

Yet there was a wee part of him that wished for her anyway, even if he didn't deserve her. He longed to hold Mery in his arms again, to taste her sweet lips upon his, to feel her warm breasts upon his chest, to sink his...

"Hey!" Thomas barked over his shoulder. "Ye'd better stir that, or 'twill burn."

Startled, Tristan blinked down at the bubbling pottage and resumed stirring.

The master cook clapped him on the shoulder, speaking for Tristan's ears alone. "Ye know, lad, if ye don't find pleasure in the cookin', all your dishes will turn bitter."

Tristan sighed and nodded.

"'Tis a woman, isn't it?"

Tristan frowned at the master cook. Was it that obvious? He supposed there was no use denying it. "Maybe."

"And she's broken your heart," Thomas guessed.

Tristan wasn't sure she'd ever claimed his heart.

"Wait." The master cook narrowed his eyes. "Not *that* woman?"

Tristan's silence was answer enough.

"Bloody hell," Thomas grumbled. "That minx of a minstrel. Did ye swive her?"

Tristan lowered guilty eyes.

Thomas glanced around for straying ears, then whispered in horror, "Not in the kitchens?"

Tristan stiffened. "Maybe."

"What the devil?" Thomas threw up his hands. "Well, that's why she's left ye then." He shook his head. "I tried to warn ye."

Tristan expected Thomas to disapprove. He'd repeated time and time again that the kitchens were no place for a woman.

What he didn't expect was that the master cook would give him advice on courting. Then again, Thomas Chalmers was the nearest thing to a father that Tristan had.

Thomas continued. "I told ye before. The kitchens are no place for a tryst."

"Actually," he murmured, "'twas *her* idea."

"What?"

"She..." Mery hadn't exactly seduced him. But making love had definitely been her plan. "She *wanted* to."

The master cook raised his brows in surprise. "Here? In the kitchens?" Thomas thought for a moment, scratching his pudgy cheek. "In that case, lad, ye should hold onto her with all your might."

Puzzled, Tristan furrowed his forehead.

Thomas patted his shoulder and explained. "Never will ye find a lass half as beautiful as that, who would o'erlook the stench o' the kitchens to swive your sorry bones." He gave Tristan a wink. "Only next time, for God's sake, take her somewhere else."

Next time. There wouldn't be a next time.

"Ye're flat again, Mery!" Harry snapped.

The rest of the minstrels trailed off at the end of the verse, leaving her flat note to echo in the great hall.

Mery sighed. "Sorry."

Harry was in an ill mood after his overindulgence last night.

She was in an ill mood as well. She hadn't seen Tristan yet today. She wasn't sure what she would say if she saw him. But after what she'd given him last night, she felt she at least deserved a "good morn."

If only she knew how he felt about her...

Was he going to cast her away, now that he'd enjoyed her charms? Did he want to meet her again for a tryst? Would he swear his undying love and ask her to marry him?

She scowled. That was unlikely. And it was foolish of her to dwell on such a ridiculous notion.

They started the *Pompae* from the beginning again. This time Mery paid close attention to her pitch. Bastian Pagez would be listening carefully to the afternoon rehearsal. Since the *Pompae equestres* had been composed by the famous George Buchanan, she didn't want to ruin a single precious note.

While the minstrels and musicians practiced in the great hall, the ambassadors met with the queen. She planned to present them with their formal commissions in the inner lodgings where Mery had seen the carved heads.

Mery hadn't forgotten the threat she'd heard the Earl of Bedford make in that very chamber. She hoped Tristan was right, that the English wouldn't dare intimidate Mary in her own castle. Still, it was worrisome knowing that the queen was, for all intents and purposes, alone with the diplomats.

What made her even more anxious was the fact that the

nobles were joining Queen Mary on a royal hunt afterward. Though Mary was robust and athletic—she enjoyed riding, hawking, archery, golf—hunting was always surrounded by mishaps. Mery was certain that many a secret murder had been concealed as an unfortunate hunting accident.

But there was little Mery could do. While the nobles were out hunting, the minstrels and musicians would be rehearsing with Pagez in the great hall.

Her only consolation was that the prince would be here at Stirling as well, safe and sound, probably indulging in an afternoon nap.

The man watched from the parapet of the castle as the hunting party rode away. Bedford was among them, going on that silly hunt with the queen.

It was a shame *he* hadn't been invited. He might have used the opportunity to his advantage. He might have grazed the queen's sleeve with an arrow or spooked her horse, just enough to make it rear and dump her onto her royal arse. She and her son had been showered with fawning praises all day yesterday. She needed a reminder that she was, after all, mortal.

In an instant, her life could be snuffed out. He could easily arrange a hunting accident, a poisoning, a slip on the stairs. If only she'd sign that document and rescind her power, the English could give her a guarantee of protection. They could ensure she would live a life free of threat...at least from Elizabeth.

He, of course, was limited by his station. He didn't have the access that an earl had. He hadn't been allowed to ride along on the hunt.

But remaining behind in the keep had one distinct advantage. The babe too had been left at Stirling under the care of the Countess of Mar.

And while he wasn't yet able to penetrate the prince's defenses, he was working his way into the confidences of his guardians. Servants loved to boast about their important duties. So he'd learned much from the Countess's rockers, who were tasked with rocking the babe's cradle. He now knew the royal schedule—when the little brat ate, slept, cried, and shat.

And he knew enough about the changing of the prince's guard to spot weaknesses, times when he might gain brief access to the babe.

It didn't hurt that Bastian Pagez had devised a complex masque following the supper tonight, complete with architectural wonders and extravagant costumes. It would add to the confusion when his opportunity for action arose.

Meanwhile, as much as it pained him to consort with the enemy, he would continue to befriend the staff and learn everything he could. Time was limited, and he was determined to succeed.

Tristan gazed into the simmering raisin custard. He reached for the cellar, picked up a fistful of salt, and held it over the pot.

Beside him, wee Easson gasped. He batted Tristan's wrist away before he could dump it into the custard. The salt scattered across the kitchen floor.

Easson's eyes were wide with mortification at what he'd done. "Sorry, sir!" he squeaked.

"Easson!" Campbell intervened, seizing the lad by an ear. "What were ye thinkin'?"

Tristan was aghast as well, not at Easson, but at himself. "Nae, 'twas my mistake. Thank ye, Easson. Ye saved the custard."

Shocked, Campbell let go of Easson's ear, and Easson stuck out his tongue at Campbell.

Tristan blew out a long breath. Bloody hell. What was *he* thinking? He would have ruined the raisin custard, and for what?

He had to stop thinking about Mery. Today came with a special challenge. Since there was no telling what kind or how many beasts the hunters would bring home, the kitchens had to prepare an assortment of sauces to go with whatever game was caught. They had to be ready for anything.

So he had to keep his mind on his work.

But it was so difficult when he kept staring at the spot on the table where he and Mery had coupled last night.

The master cook's romantic encouragements didn't help. Thomas seemed to be pleased that his apprentice had found a ladylove at long last.

But Tristan knew better. It was absurd to believe he could ever cage a wild bird like Mery Graham. She was meant to fly free. Her life was full of adventure and excitement. She couldn't possibly have room in her heart for a man who lived an uneventful life in an underground warren.

Even if she somehow did think of him as more than a warm body for a fleeting tryst...if she felt affection for him that went beyond mere desire...if she sensed, as he did, that they were somehow connected by design or destiny...how could she ever be happy, saddled with a cook's second-in-command?

Of course, he wouldn't be second forever. Thomas had hinted that, should he be promoted to the *cuisine de bouche*, cooking for the queen herself, he would bring Tristan along as master cook to the prince.

The problem was that Tristan wasn't sure he wanted the position. Cooking for royalty came with great risk. If anything untoward should befall the prince—illness, poisoning, death—all eyes would fall first on the cook.

On the other hand, if the lad survived to adulthood, Tristan would likely become the master cook to a king.

Of course, that was if he survived. Queen Mary's rival, Elizabeth, would do anything to ensure her *own* reign, including making sure the prince never achieved manhood.

He thought again about Mery's fears that there was an English plot afoot. Was it possible someone might steal into the kitchens and slip poison into the food?

He glanced around the room. He trusted his staff. They were loyal and dependable. Hell, even wee Easson had his eyes on the custard. Surely they'd never allow a stranger to violate the sanctity of the kitchens...

With one exception. That beautiful, fresh-faced minstrel lass with the voice of an angel had seemed to worm her way into everyone's hearts.

Tristan sighed. To hell with sanctity. He wished she were here now.

# ChAPTER 15

ery had to admit she may have drowned her sorrows with a wee bit more drink than was necessary. Her face felt flushed, and her knees wobbled as she wove through the mass of costumed actors. But she was on a mission. No matter how unsteady her gait, her purpose was clear. She had to unmask the English betrayer before he could do any harm.

The performance would feature a hunting allegory. While the minstrels sang the *Pompae equestres*, an actor portraying Diana the Huntress would appear, dancing with nymphs, satyrs, and men dressed as hobbyhorses in a pastoral scene.

As Mery picked up her blue velvet skirts and sidled her way through the crush of entertainers, she studied their faces. She was fairly certain that the players Pagez had hired were Scottish. But they were, after all, players. There could very well be an Englishman among them, pretending to be a *Scottish* player...pretending to be a nymph. The idea made her head spin.

They were adorned in every manner of dress. Some

wore sheer layers of green and gold sendal cut to look like foliage. Others had molded animal masks edged in black and silver. Some were bedecked with feathers, some with fur. The nymphs were clad in beautiful gowns of multi-colored silk—rose and orange and violet. The satyrs sported horns and tails. And several men rode on horses made of decorated poles.

Any one of them could be a traitor. But what troubled her most were the longbows resting against the wall.

She elbowed one of the satyrs and asked, "What are those for?"

"'Tis a hunting masque," he explained.

"But they look real."

A second satyr chimed in, "They *are* real."

Mery gasped. "Why would they be usin' real bows for a masque?"

The man portraying Diana replied. His deep voice was at odds with his feminine costume. "'Tis easier than makin' imitations."

The English consort arrived just then. The hurdy-gurdy player growled, "You only have to worry when they start using real *shafts.*"

The first satyr laughed. "If ye play badly, I may just do that."

The mincing tambor player giggled and slapped the first satyr's arm. "You wicked lad."

But Mery was serious. "What kind o' shafts will ye be usin' then?"

"Ach, they're only paper," the first satyr replied.

"*Stiffened* paper," the second satyr added.

"Stiffened," the tambor player cooed. "Ooh."

The harp player gave the tambor player a cuff on the

shoulder. "Hey, leave off the poor lads." He smirked. "They're suffering enough in their fur and feathers."

The tambor player gave the first satyr a wink. "You can fire your shaft at me any time."

The hurdy-gurdy player groaned.

Mery was too busy thinking to pay them much heed. "But paper can be sharpened to quite a fine point."

"Here," the man playing Diana replied, reaching over his back to snag a shaft out of his quiver. "See? Perfectly harmless."

Mery ran her finger over the point of the shaft. She supposed it might do some damage if it struck someone in the eye. Otherwise, it was fairly flimsy. "Ye're sure?"

The second satyr leaned forward to confide, "'Tis almost as limp as your English friend's wrist."

She ignored his comment. Though she was somewhat reassured, she still thought it would be easy enough to replace one of the paper shafts with a more deadly one.

In the end, the performance was brilliant. Mery sang in tune. The consort played well. Best of all, nobody got shot.

At least nobody who wasn't supposed to get shot got shot. There were a handful of actors dressed as beasts who served as targets for the paper arrows. The tambor player shrieked every time one of them was struck by a shaft, for they spewed blood made of red ribbons.

But aside from the shrieking, the musicians were excellent. In fact, they were so good that Harry said he was considering hiring them on permanently to accompany the minstrels. Of course, he'd forgotten they were English when he said that, and he'd been as tipsy as a cradle.

Mery too was feeling the effects of overindulgence. Instead of their usual ale, the entertainers had been treated to several wee drams o' whisky. And Mery was unaccustomed to the stuff.

By the fourth dram, she began to feel lightheaded and heavy-tongued.

By the fifth, she was giggling at everything.

By the sixth, she decided that she had to see Tristan and straighten things out between them.

Tristan scraped at the burnt residue in the bottom of the pot, silently cursing himself for ruining the chaudron sauce.

Tonight had been the busiest night of his life. It wasn't even over. The banquet had ended an hour ago. But the kitchens were still teeming with staff, cleaning and sweeping and preparing ingredients for tomorrow's dinner.

The evening had been a success. Somehow the kitchens had managed to get all the dishes out in time and at the proper temperatures. Nothing had been sent back. Nobody had complained that there wasn't enough. No one had fallen ill.

Tristan's only regret was that, in his distraction, he'd nearly mucked up so many dishes that he'd never found the time to see the woman who was the source of his distraction.

He'd hoped to hear her sing. He knew she wouldn't be here much longer. And he wanted a few pleasant memories of Mery Graham to hold onto.

Over the noise of the kitchens—banging, clattering, shouting—he suddenly heard a faint and feeble cry from the stairwell.

"Tristan?"

When he turned, he could only see her slippered feet on the stairs, peeking out from under the bottom of her blue skirts as she descended.

Casting a quick, nervous glance in the master cook's direction, he untied his apron and tossed it onto the table, then headed for the stairs.

"Tris...Tan?" What was wrong with the lass?

He frowned. Her heel slipped down a stair, and she staggered against the wall. When she came into full view, he could see at once she was drunk. Her face was flushed. Her eyes were dreamy. And her smile was wide.

She leaned happily toward him, not realizing there was one last step. When she stumbled, he caught her against his chest. Her dress slipped off of one shoulder. She gazed up at him in gushing gratitude.

"Hello, Tris."

Just then, Thomas Chalmers spotted them. "Out!" he yelled. "Both o' ye!"

Tristan could hear the snickers of the kitchen lads, who doubtless found his predicament amusing.

He took Mery by the elbow and guided her back up the stairs, past the confectionary, past the spicery, and outside. Hopefully, a long walk in the cold night air would help to sober her.

"Tristan, I mished ye."

He couldn't help but smile. "Did ye now?"

It took considerable effort to keep her walking in a straight line. But he managed, taking her to the garden outside the castle wall, where they could be alone.

Once there, he propped her against the wall.

"Ye're drunk," he informed her.

"Only a wee bit."

"What happened?"

"I looked for ye all day long," she told him. "But ye never came."

"Nae, I meant how did ye get so sotted?"

She waved away his question. "'Twas some new concoction they gave us. Whisty."

"Whisky?"

"Aye, that's the one."

Whisky wasn't new. It had been around for half a century. But if she'd never had it before, if she'd been drinking it like ale, it was no wonder she was tipsy.

"Well, ye should probably go to bed. Sleep it off."

"Nae!" she cried in desperation, pushing off from the wall to clutch him by his shirt. "I want to be with ye. I want to...swive ye again."

He swallowed back a lump in his throat. Her offer was so tempting. He could definitely swive her again. He could enjoy her like a meringue that was here for one sweet moment and then dissolved away forever. It would be heaven to make love with her once more.

She dipped her eyes and began singing softly to him. "Alas, my love, you do me wrong..."

He bit back a smile and shook his head. "Greensleeves?" It was one of the few songs he knew.

She gave him a nod and continued singing with drunken drama. "To cast me off so discourteously..."

"Shh!" he hissed, grinning and looking about for witnesses. "Lass, quiet!"

He should have known better. He should have realized hushing Mery would only make her sing all the louder.

"When I have loved you so long..."

Out of desperation, he put his fingers over her mouth to hush her.

"Delighting…" She licked between his first two fingers. "In your…" Then his second two. "Company."

She might have done more, but he snatched back his hand. Already, her tongue had shot a current of lust down his fingers, through his body, and straight to his loins.

Yet he had to resist it.

Mery wasn't the same as the other lasses he'd bedded. Other lasses he'd loved and left. But Mery was somehow different. If he coupled with her again, he wasn't so sure it would be easy to simply walk away.

"Ye know, I'm not really that sort of a man." He forced the words from his lips, justifying his reluctance to himself as well. "I can't just lie with ye one day and bid ye farewell the next. I thought I could. But I can't."

"Then don't."

He blinked. Wasn't that what he'd just said?

She placed her palms flat on his chest. "Don't bid me farewell."

He froze. What did she mean by that?

She took a moment to compose herself. She licked her lips, shook the cobwebs from her brain, smoothed his shirt, and looked him straight in the eye.

"Marry me."

# CHAPTER 16

ristan laughed. "What?"

Mery knew she was sotted to blurt out such a thing. But she was in her right mind. She just had to convince him of that. "I'm serious."

"I can't marry ye."

"Why not?"

"Ye're...drunk."

"I'm not."

He arched a dubious brow.

"I'm a wee bit drunk," she admitted. "But I have all my faculties. And I've been mullin' this over all day."

"Have ye now? A whole day?" There was still a dubious shimmer of amusement in his eyes. He wasn't taking her offer seriously.

"Aye, I have. Tell me, have ye ne'er heard o' *carpe diem?*"

"Is that a song?"

"Nae. 'Tis Latin. It means 'seize the day'."

"Seize the day."

"Take opportunity when it arises, for on the morrow,

just like that..." She tried—unsuccessfully—to snap her fingers. "It may be gone."

He hesitated. For a moment, he seemed to consider her words. But then he somberly shook his head. "Nae. Sometimes 'tis best to let...opportunity...pass ye by."

His bluntness stung. But perhaps he didn't fully understand how she felt.

"I promise ye won't regret it," she assured him. "Besides, ye'll make a fine husband. Ye've got a respectable position. Ye're the best cook I know. And ye're a better kisser than any I've had."

"Am I?" His eyes flattened then in mild irritation. "Well, that's all well and good for *ye*. But what about *me?* Would ye make a good wife? Or would ye be seizin' the day all o'er Scotland, hoppin' into other men's beds?"

Her jaw dropped in outrage. She hauled back her arm. He caught her wrist before she could clout him. She battled him for a moment for possession of her arm. But ultimately, she ceded, and he let her go.

When she finally calmed enough to speak to him, her voice trembled with hurt. "I wouldn't hop into other men's beds. I'd be faithful only to ye. How could ye think otherwise? After I gave ye my maidenhood last night and..."

He stiffened, and she suddenly realized what she'd confessed. She hadn't meant to tell him that.

"What?" he breathed. "What did ye say?"

"It doesn't matter," she said, lowering her gaze.

"Were ye... Did I..."

"Faith, it doesn't matter," she repeated. Then she captured his face between her hands and stared boldly into his eyes. "*This* is what matters. I love ye, Tristan. I know 'tis mad. I know 'tis impulsive. And aye, I've been drinkin' a wee bit. But I'm absolutely sure o' this. I've never been so sure of anythin' in my life. I love ye. I *love* ye."

She didn't give him time to answer. She surged forward and kissed him—tenderly and sweetly.

Tristan was slow to resist. Her confession had frankly shocked him. He would never have bedded Mery if he'd suspected she was a maiden. Indeed, in light of this new knowledge, he was ashamed at the careless introduction to lovemaking he'd given her. Had he been too rough, too fast, too selfish?

As far as her wanting to marry him, that was partly the whisky's influence and partly her own inexperience. She didn't understand that any man was capable of giving her pleasure. He supposed she'd learn soon enough. And when she did, she'd realize that marriage meant more than simply mating with a person who fed one's sexual appetites.

But as determined as he was to nip things in the bud, as Mery continued kissing him, his sexual appetites blossomed at an alarming pace. Her mouth tasted like honey mead, sweet and intoxicating, searing his lips while melting his heart.

It took all his will to end the kiss and set her gently but firmly away.

He almost regained control then.

Until, with no regard for where they were, she untied the laces of her stomacher and tugged it open in invitation.

"Please?" she whispered, looking up at him with passion-glazed eyes.

"Lass," he chided, tugging her stomacher back together. "Ye don't want to be doin' that."

She gave him a seductive giggle. "Aye, I do. 'Tis exactly what I want to be doin'."

She ran a fingertip down the center of his chest.

He seized her finger and shook his head. "Ye're gettin' in o'er your head."

"O' course," she said with a playful wink. "That's the only way ye can learn to swim."

"These are dangerous waters," he warned.

"I'm not afraid."

"Maybe ye should be."

"Are *ye* afraid?"

She drew her captured finger down, bringing his hand with it to rub his knuckles over the soft skin of her bosom. While he was thus distracted, she slipped her other hand down the top of his breeches, seeking the treasure within.

He grunted as her warm fingers grazed his hot flesh.

For a maiden, Mery seemed to be remarkably wise in the ways of seduction.

Aye, he was afraid. He was afraid he wasn't going to be able to resist her.

No one had ever called Mery spineless. Once she got an idea into her head, she was like a dog with a bone. And if you dared tell her she *couldn't* have a thing, you'd only make her cling to it all the more.

She needed to make love with Tristan again. Once they were flesh-to-flesh, their bodies joined, making that heavenly music together, she knew she could convince him they should be married.

So when Tristan abruptly tugged her hand out of his trews, returning it to her and choking out, "Nae, lass," it only fed her determination.

As a young woman, she'd learned the value of feminine wiles. So she looked up at him with dewy eyes and bit her lip. After a moment, her chin trembled, and her eyes filled with tears.

"Ye find me so repulsive?" she ventured.

His brow furrowed. "Ye? Nae. Not at all. Ye're... beautiful."

"Yet ye turn me away."

"'Tis only because ye don't know what ye're doin'."

She blinked. "Ye can show me. I'm a fast learner." She reached toward his breeches again.

He blocked her trespass. "That's not what I meant."

"Oh." She pretended to consider. "Am I not kissin' ye the way ye like?"

"Nae. I mean, aye, your kisses are..."

"Ye don't like brown-haired lasses," she guessed.

"I love brown-haired lasses."

"Ye do?" she asked with breathless hope.

"Aye, but..."

"But?"

"But this isn't goin' to work."

Her brow crumpled as she wailed, "'Tis because my breasts are too small, isn't it?"

He looked stunned. "What?"

She sobbed into her hands. "My Ma was right. I'll ne'er get a husband, what with breasts like a lad's."

*"What?"*

She peeked through her fingers and almost laughed aloud at the perplexed expression on his face.

"'Tis fine," she said, sniffling. "At least ye're honest."

He rattled his head as if to straighten out his warped brains.

"I suppose I don't *need* a husband," she wept. "I could always join a holy order."

"A holy...what the bloody..."

"Since I'm so undesirable as a wife." She let the tears spill down her cheeks.

As she expected, Tristan was a man who couldn't resist a lady in distress. He placed his hands on her shoulders.

"Listen to me," he said. "Ye're a beautiful lass, the most beautiful lass I've ever seen. Ye're sweet. And fun-lovin'. And bright. Your smile would light up a room. Your eyes rival the stars for shine. Any man would call himself lucky to have ye."

"Any man but ye," she said, ending on a sob.

He sighed, caught in his own net.

Behind her hands, she smiled in secret victory.

Then he said something that surprised her. "'Tis only that I care for ye too much to steal what isn't mine by rights."

He cared for her? Her heart leapt at the thought. She answered carefully. "Ye can't steal what's freely offered."

She reached up to take his wrist and turned his hand, placing a soft kiss in his palm. Then she whispered, "Make love to me."

He groaned in indecision. But she could see the temptation in his eyes. He wouldn't take much persuading.

She pressed his palm flat against her throat and urged it slowly downward, closing her eyes to revel in his arousing caress.

Finally, glancing about briefly for onlookers, he

succumbed to his desires. He kissed an impatient, seductive path down the side of her neck, over her shoulder, and across her bosom. She shivered as his touch left a trail of sparks.

He bent lower, tugging aside her linen shift with his teeth. His hand burrowed beneath her stomacher to lift her breast free of its linen confines. In the sudden cold, her nipple stiffened. But he warmed her at once, taking her into his mouth and drawing gently on her.

He ignited her nerves the way one could coax flame from a coal. Fire radiated through her entire body from that single point. She felt it heating her cheeks and burning between her thighs.

She offered him her other breast and let him suck there until she could bear to wait no longer for satisfaction.

Her hand stole inside his breeches again. He was full and firm, yet so much more vulnerable than she ever expected a man to be. When she clasped him, he growled and pushed his trews down past his hips.

His excitement increased hers. Her heart raced as she scanned the garden, wondering where they might find a place for a romantic interlude.

But it was too late for that. He desired her. Now.

He gazed at her with lust-glazed eyes.

Guessing instantly what he intended, she gathered up her skirts. He reached beneath her dress and curved his hands around her bare buttocks, lifting her up against the wall.

She clung to his shoulders and wrapped her legs around his waist. Then she took a few shuddering breaths, bracing herself for the sting of his entry.

To her amazement, this time there was no pain. Indeed,

when he sank into her body with a blissful sigh, she felt only joy.

The muscles of his arms bulged as he supported her weight in his hands and drove slowly against her. His nostrils flared at every lunge. His jaw tensed with concentration, as if he struggled to temper his passions. Watching his brow furrow as he fought to control his need heightened her desire.

She pressed wantonly against him. He rubbed across her, using the sweet friction of his thrusts to play her like a bow upon a viol. Her body sang. A warm vibration circled her head, growing in volume, surrounding her like a celestial choir. The music of their lovemaking filled her ears until the rest of the world faded away.

And then, abruptly, as if there were a rest in the music, all sound ceased. The only thing she heard was the rapid beat of her heart as her body joined with his to create that single, piercing, perfect tone.

She clenched her fists in his hair and squeezed him with her thighs. She trembled with the force of her release. With great effort, he withdrew, spilling his seed upon the ground, gasping out a final refrain that echoed in the night.

"God's truth, I love ye, Tristan," she whispered, nuzzling his neck.

What his reply would have been, she'd never know.

Suddenly, a scuffling step came from the garden path.

# CHAPTER 17

**M**ery panicked.

But Tristan, thinking quickly, set her on her feet, then guided her to a shadowy place beneath a hazel tree where they could repair their clothing.

Not a moment too soon.

The intruder entered the garden before Mery's next breath.

It was the English harp player.

She drew her brows together. What was he doing, skulking about the grounds?

As he passed by the hazel, he hissed a single word. It sounded like, "Elizabeth."

Mery blanched. Elizabeth? *Queen* Elizabeth? Her brain was still foggy from drink and swiving. But she was sure that was what he'd said.

Of course the queen couldn't possibly be here in Scotland. But why else would he call her name? Could "Elizabeth" be a code word among the English?

She watched as the harpist continued to pick his way through the garden. Again he whispered, "Elizabeth."

After he was out of hearing, she exchanged a meaningful look with Tristan, who nodded. They stealthily set out after the harpist. He proceeded past the boundary of the garden and continued on toward the stables. They couldn't follow him much farther without exposing themselves in the open field. So they watched from the safety of a hedge.

"That's the harpist. He's English. He could be the spy!" Mery whispered. "Do ye think he's gone to meet an accomplice?"

Tristan shrugged.

"Did ye hear what he was whisperin'? It sounded like…Elizabeth. The queen. 'Tis probably a secret code."

Actually, Tristan wasn't sure that was what the harpist had whispered. But it *was* suspicious that an Englishman was sneaking through the gardens of Stirling.

The harpist approached the stables. One of the doors swung open. Someone let him in and closed the door.

"See? There's his accomplice," Mery said. "I *knew* 'twas a code word." She shook her head. "But the harpist. Who would have guessed? He seemed like such a merry man." Then she sucked in a sudden breath as she realized… "Oh, nae."

"What is it?"

"Is the queen goin' ridin' on the morrow, do ye know?"

"I'm not sure."

She worried her lip. "Do ye suppose he's plottin' to put a thistle under Mary's saddle? Maybe he plans to lame her horse."

Tristan straightened as a sudden surge of male protectiveness rose up in him. It had nothing to do with his loyalty to the queen. It had everything to do with his affection for the bonnie minstrel who had just made passionate love to him, the lass who had last night given him the gift of her virginity.

"Maybe I should go and see what he's up to," he decided.

"I'll go with ye."

"'Tis too dangerous."

He should have known better than to say that...not to intrepid Mery, who had faced down Thomas Chalmers, the master cook. Her hackles rose at once, and she arched a challenging brow. He knew there was no arguing her out of going now.

He sighed. "Will ye at least let me go first?"

"If ye like. But I'll be right behind ye."

He raised his own sardonic brow. "Seizin' the day?"

She smiled. "Seizin' your arse."

He grinned.

They should have returned to the castle. What happened next was an unfortunate and embarrassing mishap.

As it turned out, the harpist had not gone to the stables to put a thistle under the queen's saddle. When Tristan yanked open the door in the hopes of catching the villain in the act of laming a horse, he caught him instead in the act of swiving an alto.

Behind him, Mary gasped. "Elspeth?"

The harpist squeaked in alarm, turning a furious red as he tried to pull his trews back up over his naked buttocks. "What the devil?"

Tristan figured out at once what had gone wrong. But Mery hadn't quite put it all together yet.

"Elspeth," Mery demanded, "are ye givin' aid to the enemy?"

"Well, I *was*," Elspeth complained, snapping her skirts back down, "until *ye* came stormin' through the door."

"How could ye?" Mery asked. "How could ye betray the queen and—"

"Lass," Tristan said with a grimace.

"Endanger the life o' the prince when—"

"Lass."

"Ye were just singin' her praises—"

"Lass!"

"What!"

"'Elspeth,'" he told her.

"What?"

"He was callin' 'Elspeth'."

Mery only stared at him.

"Besides, Mery Graham," Elspeth said, "what are *ye* doin' out here with the cook?"

Mery started sputtering.

Tristan didn't want to make the situation any worse. So he grabbed Mery's hand and tugged her toward the door. "My sincerest apologies for the interruption," he said to the unhappy couple. "'Twas a grievous mistake. Carry on. Forget we e'er... Good night."

He closed the door gently behind them.

"Oh dear," Mery said when she finally caught on. "They weren't plottin' against the queen."

"Nae."

They started walking back to the castle. Mery was silent at first, no doubt mortified by what she'd done.

But her mortification didn't last long.

"Ach," she said with a snicker. "Did ye see the look on the poor harpist's face?"

He *had* looked rather comical and redder than a cherry

tart. "Like he'd been caught with his trews down?"

She giggled. "And Elspeth." She clucked her tongue. "No doubt she'll be drownin' me out all week for interruptin' her." A moment later, she sighed. "Well, one can't be too careful."

"Though from now on," he suggested, "maybe ye should stay away from the whisky."

She gave him a playful elbow. "'Twasn't *all* bad."

A crooked grin slipped onto his face. "True."

"So, Tristan MacKenzie," she said, slipping her arm through his, "what about that marriage?"

Misgiving dropped over him like a cold linen bed sheet. He knew, now that she'd given him her virginity, she expected his commitment in return. She'd even confessed her love.

But those words were spoken under the influence of drink. He didn't dare offer himself to her. She wanted his heart now. But on the morrow she'd likely break it.

"Let's see how ye feel about it after this is all over," he said, "when ye're ready to travel on. And when ye haven't been drinkin'."

She gave him a coy smile. "If I'm drunk, 'tis only on your love."

He planted a fond but carefully dispassionate kiss on her mouth. Then he escorted her through the garden to the great hall. Harry was there, gathering the minstrels to return to their lodgings and wondering if anyone knew where Elspeth was.

# CHAPTER 18

**DECEMBER 19**

Mery and Elspeth had come to an agreement, whispering back and forth as they made their way up the esplanade to the castle. They'd decided never to speak of what had transpired last night. After all, it would only upset Harry, especially if found out young Mery, whom he treated almost like a daughter, had been in the garden alone with Tristan MacKenzie.

She smiled at the memory.

She *had* been rather drunk. But she wouldn't change a thing. She still meant what she'd said. Mery intended to wed Tristan MacKenzie.

Halfway up the hill, she began to chew at her lip.

What if he didn't love her?

She'd been reckless with her virginity. Once again, she'd leaped before she looked.

But she had to believe fate wouldn't steer her wrong.

Fate had delivered her into the band of minstrels. And if it hadn't been for them, she would never have met Tristan.

If Tristan *did* marry her, Harry would be unhappy to lose her. But he'd understand, once he knew the truth. He'd always said life on the road was no place for a maid or a married woman. That's why she'd let him believe she was a childless widow like the other women in the group, well-suited to a life of wandering.

She wouldn't tell Harry yet. After all, she still had to wait one more day to finalize the decision, at Tristan's insistence.

It felt like an eternity. And patience was not one of Mery's virtues.

They were drawing near to Stirling when she noticed a crowd gathered at the gates. The castle folk were watching the preparations for this evening's spectacle. Mery followed their gaze.

In the valley below the keep sat a miniature mock fortress. She'd never seen such a thing. It was the perfect replica of a castle, constructed out of wood. She grinned in delight as the musical entourage around her exclaimed.

"Look at the towers!" Ginny the soprano squealed.

"That must have cost a few shillings," the hurdy-gurdy player grumbled.

"I heard they're goin' to destroy it," said Davy the bass, sounding pleased at the prospect.

"But it's so precious," the tambor player complained, clucking his tongue. "Can't you imagine little faeries living in it?"

The viol player rolled his eyes.

Even the lutist, a man of few words, gushed, "It's enchanting."

"Well, don't get attached," the hurdy-gurdy man told her. "It'll be in splinters by the morrow."

The harpist elbowed him. "You don't need to spoil it for her."

Mery blinked, alarmed. "Splinters? What do ye mean?"

The hurdy-gurdy player looked down at her with an air of superiority. "I'm not at liberty to say."

Mery resisted the urge to level him with a punch to his cocky chin. Instead, she shrugged. "I'm certain 'twill be safe, whatever they've planned." She had to assume Pagez wouldn't do anything to endanger the queen.

"Safe?" The hurdy-gurdy man guffawed. "*Safe?*"

Mery would have liked to throttle him with his own hurdy-gurdy. For once, Harry prevented her from following her instincts.

"Come along, ducklin's," he called out. "Let's break our fast and quickly. We've got things to do."

Because there were so many preparations being made in the great hall, the minstrels and consort were fed in the small chamber above the kitchens again. There they feasted on squares of pandemain with tangy apricot preserves, washing them down with watered ale.

Mery licked her fingers, deciding that after they were wed, she'd have Tristan make these for her every day.

"Good morn."

Mery jumped guiltily, clapping her hand to her bosom. Everyone else returned Tristan's greeting.

He addressed the group. "I'm to tell ye that Bastian Pagez wishes ye to report to him in the inner close immediately after ye break your fast. He has..." Mery detected a small shudder go through him. "Costumes for everyone."

Tristan was not looking forward to this dinner. Not only were Pagez's serving instructions specific and complicated. But he was going to have to follow them, dressed in the most ridiculous costume he'd ever seen.

As he'd discovered from the previous night's banquet, a satyr was apparently part man and part goat. So he'd be wearing furry brown trews, boots, and a sash that barely covered his chest.

He only wished Mery wouldn't be there to see him. He suddenly cared a great deal what she thought of him. Her costume would probably be beautiful. But his promised to be humiliating. One look at him, and she'd withdraw that marriage offer as fast as she'd issued it.

Which, to be honest, was fine.

After all, he had no business being married.

He'd spent half the night imagining the joy of having Mery for a wife. He'd thought about making passionate love to her every evening. He'd envisioned waking to her glorious smile every morn. Hell, he'd even created images in his mind of what their children would look like.

But it had been an exercise in futility. He'd come to that conclusion this morn, as he realized how impossible a relationship with Mery would be.

Now that she was sober, she'd remember there was a big, wide world out there yet for her to explore...and men a lot more expert at lovemaking than he was. She deserved someone who excited her. Someone who could take her on impulsive adventures. Someone who wasn't confined to the kitchens, obliged to perform at the whim of royals.

Still, for the time being, he'd put on a brave face. As Mery had advised, he'd seize his opportunity. They may not have tomorrow. But they had today. And from what he'd heard, it promised to be an exciting day indeed.

"Oh, sir!" Mery suddenly called, addressing him with a secret wink. "Some of us were wonderin' about the wee castle in the yard."

"Aye?" He'd seen the fortress in its various stages of construction over the last several weeks.

"*Some* people," she said pointedly, "are sayin' they'll be destroyin' it."

"Aye, so I've heard."

"Truly?" She looked crestfallen. "But why?"

"From what I understand, they've arranged a mock battle."

"A battle?" Harry asked.

"With crossbows and spears?" the harpist asked, rubbing his hands together.

"I suppose so." He didn't want to reveal Pagez's secret, even if half the castle already knew.

Mery frowned. "And what else?"

"Horses," one of the male minstrels guessed. "They've got to have horses."

"Hopefully more convincin' than the hobbyhorses they had last night," another minstrel added with a chortle.

The hurdy-gurdy player straightened with authority. "They aren't using players at all. They're using real soldiers."

Elspeth gasped. "What? Where did ye hear that?"

He gave her a self-important sniff. "I have my sources."

Before panic could ensue, Tristan added, "Well, aye,

they'll be real soldiers. But they won't be usin' real force."
At least he hoped they wouldn't.

"I heard they have a catapult," one of the minstrels volunteered.

"A catapult!" another minstrel cheered.

The rest of the men joined in with chuckles of approval.

"I saw gunpowder," the harpist volunteered.

The room gave a collective gasp.

The violist looked grim, as usual. "Is there to be a war?"

"Oh, nae," Tristan assured him. "'Tis only for show."

He could see all this speculation would only cause trouble. So he decided to cut it short. "Pagez can probably tell ye the truth of it. So if ye've finished your meal…"

The women looked worried. The men were grinning like madmen, slapping one another on the back as they left, almost as if the bloodthirsty fools were marching off to war.

Mery came up beside him. "Gunpowder?" she whispered.

"Oh, that's not all," Tristan murmured, eager to share the exciting news with her. He leaned in close. "Can ye keep a secret?"

She nodded.

"They've got guns and cannon…and fireworks."

To his disappointment, her eyes didn't light up in excitement. They widened in fear.

"Faith, that's how they're goin' to do it," she breathed.

"Do what?"

"The English. That's how they're plannin' to hurt the prince. They're goin' to blow him up."

Tristan scowled. He thought that was very unlikely. The entire event had been planned for weeks by the queen's own John Chisholm and two expert gunners, Charles Bordeaux and James Hector. All three were loyal Scots.

"No doubt the prince will be kept well away from the fireworks," he assured her. "All that noise and smoke would make a bairn cry."

But despite his assurances, there was a wee, determined furrow between her brows. And suddenly Tristan knew he'd made a mistake in telling the intrepid lass anything.

"Don't ye even think of it, lass."

"Think o' what?"

"Whate'er ye're thinkin' o' doin'."

"I wasn't thinkin' o' doin' anything."

"The hell ye weren't." He could well imagine her snooping around the stores of gunpowder with a lit match.

"The prince's welfare is at stake," she argued.

"And just what do ye intend to do about it? Do ye know anythin' about fireworks?"

Too late, he realized that, to Mery's ears, his words didn't sound like a warning. They sounded like a challenge.

There wasn't much that Mery would let stand in her way. That included Tristan's grim warning. Which was how, just after Pagez's rehearsal, she ended up at the fenced enclosure adjacent to the miniature castle. The soldiers were there, preparing for the upcoming spectacle.

She peeked inside the yard. To her surprise, just inside the gate, speaking to a soldier, was the tambor player. She quickly dropped out of sight behind the fence of wooden stakes.

What was he doing here? Could the tambor player be the English spy? Was he planning to steal some of the weapons or commandeer the artillery?

She strained her ears to listen, but could only hear one side of the conversation.

"I've never seen so many big guns!" he exclaimed.

The soldier's reply was muffled.

"Well, they seem powerful to me," the tambor player said. "You must be quite fearless to withstand all the smoke and noise."

She couldn't hear the answer.

"What's this one?"

There was a pause while the soldier explained.

"Zounds! And how does it work exactly?"

The soldier continued mumbling.

Finally, the tambor player sighed. "You know, I've always admired soldiers. You lads are so brave and strong."

This was followed by a lot of quiet exchanges and giggling by the tambor player.

Then he asked, "But you're quite sure they're harmless?" He gave an audible shiver. "I'm certain tonight I shall be absolutely cowering in fright."

The soldier mumbled for a long while.

Then the tambor player replied, "Ooh, fireworks? In that case, I may well need a cuddle to calm me down."

Mery rubbed impatiently at the crease between her brows. Apparently, the mincing tambor player was plotting, not to hurt the prince, but to feed his own romantic appetites.

At least he'd done her one favor. He'd completed her investigation for her. The soldier had listed the armaments and decreed that the fireworks were indeed harmless. She hoped he was right.


Tristan had never been more irked in his life as he trudged up the kitchen stairs. Bloody hell, he was a cook, not a player. He felt half naked in the damned satyr costume. Nobody had warned him that it came with horns and a tail. Worse, the master cook hadn't been able to stop laughing once he caught sight of Tristan in the kitchens.

He adjusted the sash once more, tugging at it in the hopes he could increase its width to completely cover his chest, if not his entire head. But his efforts were in vain. His only consolation was that he wasn't alone. Eleven servers, dressed just like him, shared in his misery.

They gathered in the staging area, where Pagez was peering through the curtain into the great hall. There was a large platform in its midst. While the guests watched in awe, a round table was assembled upon the platform by means of an ingenious mechanical device with gears and levers.

Though Tristan couldn't see the performers, he heard the music begin. It was a painful reminder that Mery was going to see him like this. He pulled one last time at the sash, to no avail.

Then Pagez handed him a lit torch and a whip.

He shook his head. This experience was definitely going to scar him for life.

The first course was ready to be wheeled out on its table by the other satyrs. So when the curtain parted, he stepped into the great hall, cursing under his breath and cracking his whip to clear the way.

# CHAPTER 19

Mery couldn't wait for Tristan to see her in her Nereid costume. She felt like a real goddess as they began the strains of Buchanan's masterpiece, an offering of gifts from the rustic gods to Mary and her son.

She'd never performed in a costume before. Normally, men played all the parts in a masque, even the female roles. In Pagez's production, everyone took part. The musicians were dressed as maidens. Even the servants were costumed as nymphs and satyrs, naiads and fauns. Mery supposed the nobles could hardly frown on such a thing, considering the queen regularly disguised herself in men's clothing.

Mery was clad in a robe made of layers of white silk edged with gold. Her hair, hanging in long, loose waves, was covered by a headdress of red coral. Her feet were wickedly bare.

She watched with amazement as a round table seemed to magically assemble itself on top of the stage. The guests too were awestruck as they were directed to their places.

She missed her entrance as the sudden crack of a whip startled her. When she saw who wielded the whip, it took her a full phrase to catch up with the other singers.

It was Tristan. He looked splendid. The light of his torch cast a golden glow over him, accentuating his scowling features and the planes of his half-bared chest. And the way he flexed his arm, cracking his whip, made her knees go weak.

Despite wearing horns and a tail, he was surely the most alluring beast she'd ever seen. Her skin tingled as she thought about pressing her cheek against his naked shoulder. Her blood warmed as she imagined wrapping her bare legs around his fur-clad hips.

She had a hard time looking away from him as he strode forward, clearing the way for the large wheeled table that was dragged into the room. Six nymphs sat atop the table, handing out heaping platters of food to the satyrs, who served the guests.

The entertainers continued to perform during the meal. Some of the nymphs and satyrs joined in, leaping and twirling and wagging their tails in a playful dance designed by Bastian Pagez.

While they sang, Mery's stomach growled at the sumptuous smells as the dishes were presented. Hen with lemon. Mutton pies. Baked venison with redcurrants. Pigs' cheeks with marmalade. Roast goose with gooseberries. Peacock with ginger sauce.

Still, she couldn't decide which looked more appetizing—the fat roasts served with their rich, glistening sauces or the well-muscled satyr directing the service.

She tried to catch Tristan's eye, staring at him with an

intensity that should have bored a hole in him. But he seemed oblivious. He continued to frown at the table, almost as if he'd like to overturn it. She wondered why he was upset.

Trouble was brewing.

Tristan wasn't sure what was wrong. His first thought was that the English didn't like the food. Maybe it was too spicy. Maybe it was too bland. Maybe they didn't care for goose. Or porpoise. Or sand eels.

He'd drawn closer to the table to see if he could figure out what the problem was when he overheard an alarming statement.

In a way, he was relieved. It wasn't the food after all, but the masque they objected to. To a certain extent, he had to agree. Being served by half-nude men dressed as nymphs and satyrs had to be unappetizing.

Still, he thought it was the epitome of rudeness when some of the Englishmen, claiming they'd been insulted, sat to face away from the entertainment.

He withdrew to join Pagez in the adjoining chamber.

Pagez was muttering French curses. "Those English imbeciles," he spat. "They are acting childish. To take offense at such a thing…" He looked at Tristan. "Pah! Take them more wine. They will soon forget their anger."

Tristan wondered. He'd overheard one Englishman say to another that, were he the queen, he would have stabbed Bastian Pagez for giving such offense. For that, and for Tristan's own reasons, he'd just as soon not return to the great hall.

During the whole first course, he hadn't had the courage

to look once at Mery Graham. Hearing her was bad enough. Considering his appearance, he was surprised she was able to sing at all without choking on laughter. He didn't know how much longer he could avoid her gaze. He wanted nothing more than to take off his bloody horns and tail and crawl back down to the kitchens.

"What's wrong?" Mery whispered to the English musicians. "Why are they upset?"

"'Tis the tails," the violist explained.

"The tails?"

The hurdy-gurdy player leaned forward and growled, "Don't pretend you don't know what they say about the English."

"What?" Mery asked. She had no idea what he was talking about.

"That we have tails?" the tambor player said, stifling a giggle.

"What?"

The lute player placed a sympathetic hand on Mery's forearm. "You've never heard?"

The harpist offered, "'Tis an insult, an old story that the English have tails."

Mery blinked. It was the first she'd heard of it. "What's that got to do with us?"

The hurdy-gurdy player snorted. "Didn't you see what the satyrs were doing, waving their tails in the guests' faces, taunting them?"

She hadn't. Tristan, at least, hadn't been doing that. "But I'm sure 'twasn't meant to be an insult. 'Twas only in fun."

"Tell that to Hatton." The hurdy-gurdy player nodded to

one of the Englishmen, who had turned to sit backwards, facing away from the entertainers.

Mery narrowed her eyes at the fellow. Even facing away, his displeasure was evident in the bristling of his shoulders. Could he be the English villain sent to influence the queen by "unsavory means"? If he was so easily riled, perhaps he was the type of man who could be persuaded to violence.

Fortunately, the third course was served, not by the satyrs, but by means of a conduit down which the dishes were delivered. This seemed to mollify the diners for the moment. As plates of roasted snipes, baked carp, and stewed sparrows made their way across the table, the minstrels sang again.

The piece was another by Buchanan, the *Pompae Deorum Rusticorum*. The lyrics of the song likened the queen to both King Arthur and the goddess Astrea. Like Arthur, Mary was apparently the bringer of the golden age and the fulfiller of Merlin's prophecy. Like Astrea, she was the restorer of peace and harmony.

Even as Mery joyfully expounded on the queen's virtues in song, she couldn't help but wonder what the foreign ambassadors thought of this lofty comparison. Surely the English, who believed Elizabeth was the rightful heir to the throne, would argue that the Scottish queen thought rather highly of herself.

Mery glanced at the diplomats seated around the table. No doubt they also bristled at the idea of the table representing the Round Table of King Arthur, clearly indicating the rest of them were all equals. The Earl of Bedford, in particular, must be insulted by the insinuation that Queen Mary was the figurehead who would unite the countries.

At least they were eating well, she thought. It was hard

to be too angry when one was dining on such elegant fare.

Before the fourth course, the minstrels performed again as a great painted globe was lowered from the ceiling. It slowly split open to reveal a beautiful rosy-cheeked child dressed like an angel.

Mery stole a glance at the wee prince, who stared up at the spectacle in wonder from the Countess of Mar's lap, waving his tiny arms. Her heart melted at the sight. Suddenly she was struck with an overwhelming desire to have a child of her own. Nae, she corrected, a child of her and Tristan's making.

That instant, as if he came to do her bidding, Tristan marched out like an ancient god, bearing a platter of baked trout on one broad shoulder. Mery's cheeks flamed as she admired his half-naked body. She wickedly wondered what the odds were of convincing Tristan to make love to her tonight in his satyr costume.

More and more dishes arrived. Veal with orange. Stewed capons. Roasted beef. Lamprey pottage. Pigeon pie. Mery licked her lips, idly wondering if she'd grow fat, wed to a man who regularly served up such rich fare. She smiled, deciding she'd definitely have to taste everything he prepared to be sure it was fit for the royals.

The more she thought about it, the more certain she became that marriage to Tristan MacKenzie was inevitable, a quirk of fate that was meant to be.

Tristan could resist no longer. While the nymphs twirled about to the minstrels' song, he stole a glance at Mery.

She was transformed. If she'd been bonnie before, now she was radiant. She looked like a goddess plucked straight from the sea. Her dark honey hair hung in glossy ocean-washed waves, crowned by sprigs of red coral. Her costume, made of nearly transparent layers of sheer white, flowed around her like kelp in the current. When she moved, the edges of her gown flashed with ribbons of metallic gold.

But what made the breath catch in his throat was the sight of her bare feet beneath the gown. The whole represented Mery Graham perfectly—by all appearances an ethereal goddess, and yet an innocent child beneath. Her toes peeped out like perfect pearls, and he longed to kiss each one.

His chest swelled with desire and then sank with despair.

In another world, they might have courted and married. In another time, they might have made a home and children. Anywhere else, they might have had a chance to make a future together. Just not here.

But maybe Mery was right. Maybe they were meant to grasp happiness in what short time they had. If that was so, then he intended to fill every spare moment until her departure, worshiping the beautiful goddess with the adorable toes.

This was the chance the man had been waiting for. Soon there would be time to do what needed to be done.

Clearly the arrogant queen had no intention of bending in the least when it came to her son's claim to the throne. She'd repeatedly ignored Bedford's overtures regarding the treaty. The diffident earl had been unable to secure even five minutes with her alone.

By her self-aggrandizing displays, it was obvious she deemed her line superior to that of her cousin Elizabeth. And it was evident from the rude and insulting dance she'd allowed Pagez to orchestrate that she bore no respect whatsoever for the English.

It was time for sterner measures.

It was time to make history.

The fact that Christopher Hatton had caused a stir over the entertainment was convenient. There was already tension in the air. That kind of distraction made his task easier.

One more dramatic incident should buy him enough time. And those wheels were already set in motion.

He'd accomplished the first part while everyone's eyes were fixed on the globe being lowered from the ceiling. It was simple work to locate one of the key supports under the stage and the heavy iron bolt that held it in place. While the nobles were raving in awe over the child-angel descending from the heavens—no doubt to bestow a godly crown upon the Scottish pretenders—he twisted out the bolt and dropped it onto the ground.

The effect was not immediate. But soon after, just as the fifth course was about to be served, the support, detached from the rest of the structure, began to bend under the weight of the guests. He watched as the platform gradually listed to one side.

The nobles exclaimed as they felt the ground shift beneath them. Some popped up in panic, which only made the stage sink diagonally that much faster. Dishes slid across the table, and servants scrambled to catch them before they fell.

In the ensuing chaos, he slipped over to the serving

table. It was laden with sweets, pastries, and bottles of sack from Spain, the final course of the banquet.

From Helen Little, the prince's nursemaid, he'd learned that each night after supper the prince was given a warm posset of watered wine in a small gold cup. She'd told him it helped the child sleep.

He saw the cup upon the table. His mouth curved up in a grim smile. Tonight it would indeed make the prince sleep—far better than he'd ever slept before.

Slipping poison into the cup was child's play. Since he'd come to Scotland, he'd worn a poison ring containing deadly dwale in the event such an opportunity should arise. He simply strolled up to the table while the others were tending to the upset guests, uncorked the vial of the dwale extract and emptied three drops into the gold cup. It wouldn't take much. Two drops could easily kill a larger child. The poison dissolved invisibly into the watered wine. Not that it mattered to a babe, but its taste was also undetectable.

Once consumed, the dwale would take effect in perhaps an hour or so. By that time, no one would be able to trace from whence the poison had come. Indeed, poison might not even be suspected. The prince would suffer from vertigo, vision problems, thirst, and the loss of his voice. But those signs would hardly be noticed in an infant. By morn, he would be dead. And babes died in their beds all the time of mysterious causes.

He closed the ring and backed away from the table. Furrowing his brow into an expression of earnest concern, he scurried over to the broken stage to see how he could be of help.

# CHAPTER 20

ery's heart dropped when she saw the stage collapse. Her first instinct was to save the prince. Indeed, she'd hurried halfway to his side when she saw the wee bairn was already well defended. Not only had the queen swept him up in her arms, but at least half a dozen noblewomen made a circle around him. And *they* were swiftly surrounded by a protective layer of Scottish guards.

She guessed Tristan was right. Nothing could happen to the prince when so many loyal subjects were willing to lay down their lives for the bairn.

As it turned out, no one was hurt. Despite her concern that foul play might be involved, it seemed unlikely. One of the bolts securing the braces beneath the stage had simply come loose. She supposed with the shifting of weight as the servers moved around, it was inevitable that at some point the braces would bend out of place and come crashing down.

Tristan was quick to direct the staff in reseating the startled guests. Since the stage had fully collapsed, the serving table could no longer be drawn up in the same manner as before. It was instead moved to the space beside the musicians and minstrels, where the servers could deliver the dishes by hand.

Mery's gaze slipped more than once to the table full of sweets. There were glazed chuet pastries full of mince, lovely spiced puddings, a velvety white cheese tarte, slices of gingerbread, squares of marchpane in vivid colors, and those lovely little meringue clouds. It was tempting to steal one. She bit her lip.

But just then she glanced up to see Tristan on the other side of the table, his arms crossed sternly over his chest, his brow fixed in a warning scowl as he gazed at her.

She caught her breath. Suddenly the sweets didn't look half as appetizing as the satyr standing guard over them. She let her eyes course lazily down his body, taking in every delicious contour.

His scowl deepened, and his nostrils flared. He might be staring at her in disapproval, but there was no mistaking the smoldering heat in his eyes. He wanted her as well. Aye, she thought, tonight for certain, there would be an historic coupling for the first time between a satyr and a Nereid.

He averted his gaze then, which was probably wise. Those fur breeches were doing a poor job of hiding his incriminating interest. And he was obviously too preoccupied to sneak off to a dark corner just now.

But the thought of the possibilities heated her blood. She reached for her cup of cider, hoping to quench her thirst. But it was empty. She cast about, looking for something to drink.

The pitcher of ale was gone. The nobles had been served bottles of sherry from the serving table. But a few stray cups appeared to have been left behind. Mery supposed they might be spares. She sidled up to the table and peered at their contents. Too thirsty to care much whether they held rare sherry or watered ale, she glanced about to be sure no one was watching and then snatched up the smallest one.

She tossed it back quickly and replaced the cup. The taste was disappointing, like very watery wine. But it served its purpose. It quenched her thirst.

And not a moment too soon. To ease the rattled guests, Harry started the music immediately. The final piece was a triumphant celebration of peace and harmony. Between the uplifting song and the delectable assortment of sweets, no one could remain upset for long.

Finally the banquet was over, and the guests withdrew from the great hall. The minstrels and musicians chattered about the spectacle yet to come.

"I'd advise you to stay well away from the battle," the harp player was telling Elspeth.

The lutist murmured, "Perhaps we should travel on to the next town before it starts."

The hurdy-gurdy player snorted. "I'm not sure even the next town is safe. Did you see how much artillery they've got?"

The tambor player gasped and slapped his arm. "Stop it. You're scaring him."

Christopher the tenor agreed. "Zounds, you're scarin' *me.*"

Harry chuckled. "I'm sure Pagez knows what he's doin'. He's done such entertainments before in France."

"Aye, so I've heard," said the harpist. "His spectacle in Beauvieux was legendary."

"Beauvieux?" the hurdy-gurdy player barked. "Never heard of it."

The harpist winked at Elspeth. "That's because 'tisn't there anymore."

Mery laughed.

The tambor player smacked the harpist's arm. "You are such a rogue!"

"If ye're afraid," teased Davy the bass, "maybe ye should scurry home to England."

Anyone else might have bristled at the insult. But musicians were an easygoing lot. They laughed along with the minstrels as they packed their instruments away.

The violist seemed unsure. "I plan to stay indoors. I've no desire to see soldiers blast each other to bits."

Elspeth agreed, which made the harpist unhappy, until she rather pointedly declared she planned to go for a moonlit walk in the garden instead.

Mery frowned, mentally crossing off that trysting spot for her and Tristan.

"Well," the tambor player announced, wiggling his brows suggestively, "I'm off to find a soldier to make my *own* fireworks."

The hurdy-gurdy player groaned.

While the musicians continued to banter, impatient Mery slipped away to search for her satyr.

She spied him carrying a heavy tray across the wooden bridge to the kitchens. Silently, she crept up behind him. Then, unable to resist, she yanked his tail.

"Shite!" he hissed, almost dropping the tray.

Despite Mery's playful grin, he gave her an annoyed glare.

"What?" she asked.

"Don't do that," he grumbled.

"What—this?" She gave his tail another tug.

He made a sound that was half squeak, half growl.

She giggled.

"Ye needn't mock me," he groused. "I've had my fill o' shame already this eve."

"Shame?" She skipped around him until she blocked his forward path.

He scowled at her. "Go on. Laugh."

"Laugh?" She let her gaze drizzle as slowly as honey over his luscious contours. Then she murmured, "That's the last thing I want to do." She bit her lip and ran her fingertip along his bare forearm. "Indeed, ye've put me in a mind to seize the night, satyr. How soon can ye get away?"

"Are ye teasin' me?"

Her eyelids dipped with desire. "Do I look like I'm teasin' ye?"

He waved to his horned crown in disbelief. "Like this?"

"Oh, aye." She gave him a sultry smile. "I insist. I've ne'er swived a satyr before."

"Ye've only swived a man twice."

"True."


Tristan couldn't believe she was serious. But the lass seemed sincere.

Ever since he'd seen her in the filmy white gown and coral crown, he'd decided she was the most comely lass in all of Stirling. He longed to delve his hands into her long, flowing tresses. And the glimpse of her pale, bare feet had filled him with such desire that he could hardly focus his thoughts.

The corner of his lip curved up as he realized this lovely sea goddess actually wanted him, horns and all.

"I suppose the kitchen lads can do the rest," he said, handing off the tray to a passing servant.

"Where can we go?" she breathed.

"I know just the spot." He took her hand.

Everyone was gathering at the eastern wall of the castle for the fireworks display. No one would venture to the west kitchen gardens, not at this time of night.

They stole through the moonlight past the tunnel of the north gate.

She shivered. He remembered she was wearing no shoes. And her sheer gown couldn't be keeping her very warm in the brisk December air.

He paused, sweeping her up in his arms to carry her through the garden gate. She wrapped her arms around his neck and purred against his throat.

Closing the gate behind them with his boot, he strode down the path, past bare-limbed fruit trees, finding the wooden bench against the far wall. There he set her down.

"Come, satyr," she beckoned, patting the bench beside her.

He shook his head. He'd been thinking about this all evening.

He knelt before her on one knee and captured her right foot in his hands. As he lifted it, she tipped back onto her elbows, gazing at him in curious wonder.

Her foot was cold, so he warmed it between his palms. Then he pressed the pads of his thumbs into her arch, kneading her like fine bread.

She sighed in pleasure, letting her head fall back. Her coral crown glowed in the moonlight, contrasting with the lush bronze waves of her hair.

Then he lowered his head to worship her precious toes, kissing the tip of each, one by one.

Low in her throat, she made a sound that was part pleasure, part amusement.

He repeated the ritual for her other foot. But this time, he slid his hand up the back of her calf.

She gasped in delight and recoiled just a little as he grazed the sensitive skin behind her knee. Watching the lust play over her features, he moved his fingers to the inside of her knee and pressed ever-so-gently.

She opened her knees, and he continued his pursuit, gliding the back of his knuckles up along her thigh. She sucked a breath slowly between her teeth, and he smiled in satisfaction.

"Lie back, lass," he softly bade her.

She eased off of her elbows. Her hands, however, were clenched into fists.

"Are ye afraid?" he asked.

He must have pricked her pride, for she forced her fists to relax. "Nae."

Inch by inch, he slipped his fingers under the wispy layers of her gown and up the inside of her silky thighs. He spread her limbs with sensuous stealth.

When he contacted the warm, downy place between her legs, she moaned. The soft sound sent a jolt of lust through him. He strained against the confines of his breeches. But he had to save his own need for later. First he wanted to bring her pleasure.

Wary of his sharp horns, he pushed her gown out of the

way and eased his head forward. Where his fingers had traced a path, he let his tongue follow.

This time he knew it wasn't fear, but desire, that clenched her fists. He chuckled against her flesh.

When he parted her nether lips, she stiffened. And when he blew a warming breath across her, she groaned. But when he lowered his head to kiss her, she tangled her fingers in his hair as if to ensnare him.

She was savory-sweet upon his tongue, like a rare and exotic dish he'd never tried before. He forced himself to sample her as one would a sweetmeat, in small and delicate nibbles. But what he longed to do was feast upon her with an unearthly craving.

# CHAPTER 21

Once when she was little, Mery had nearly been struck by lightning. That was how she felt now. Every inch of her felt roused and full of current. His breath sent shivers along her skin. His tongue made every nerve come alive.

She was beyond thought, beyond reason. He made her feel like a goddess.

She arched her hips up, wishing to be closer to her worshiping satyr, yearning to give him every bit of her.

He answered her, laving and drawing and tugging at her flesh until she could do nothing but roll her head in delicious agony.

Still feasting on her, he climbed her ribs with his fingertips, nudging under her breasts. Just as she thought she could reach no greater height, he sucked at the very core of her and tenderly caught her nipples between his fingers.

With a sharp cry, she exploded into a thousand fragments, like the lightning-struck pine beside her had done all those years ago.

Wave after wave of joy pulsed through her. It seemed as if the night flooded with starlight.

And then it slowly dimmed, leaving her in the glowing garden with her beloved satyr snuggled between her legs.

After a moment, she felt him stir. With a satiated smile, she twined her fingers around his horns.

"Oh, my satyr," she whispered, "will ye mate with me now?"

His answer was an eager growl.

Heaving himself up on his powerful arms, he moved over her until he blocked out the sky. She slipped her hands beneath his sash to caress his firm, muscled chest.

Supporting himself on one arm, he used the other to untie his breeches, freeing his full and ready staff.

With a gasp of anticipation, she wrapped her legs around his furry haunches.

Locking gazes with her, he slowly slid forward. She gulped. Though his arms shook with restraint, he took his time, forcing her to feel his penetration, inch by breathtaking inch.

When he finally lodged fully within her, she squeezed her heels into his buttocks, grinding her hips up against his.

The furrow between his brows might have been pain or pleasure. For her, every thrust was like a delicious lash of his whip, caressing her with tender lust, driving her mad with longing.

The chill of the night disappeared as their bodies met again and again in the feverish dance. He panted with exertion. She gasped with elation. The music of their mating grew more complex as they soared over passionate passages and delved into deeper harmonies. And then they reached a pitch of such volume that she feared the whole universe would hear.

With a great muffled groan, he bucked forward into her with satyr-like force. But she rode him like a commanding goddess, arching through the heavens and holding tightly onto him with her legs until they were both spent and shivering.

Their breath made mist upon the chill air, but Mery was far from cold. He had warmed her to the core.

She gazed up at him with adoration. His horns were askew, and she giggled, tugging them off of him. Somehow her coral crown had fallen as well, and he retrieved it from the ground, placing it on his own head.

Suddenly they heard distant gunfire.

"The fireworks!" she eagerly cried, pushing up to her elbows.

He shrugged. "They couldn't rival ours."

She grinned. "True." Nonetheless, she'd love to see the spectacle. She'd never seen fireworks before.

He seemed to read her mind. He carefully withdrew from her and tied up his breeches. "But ye don't want to miss it. Pagez has promised the best display ever."

Her eyes lit up as she straightened her gown and let him tug her to her feet.

They hurried from the garden, past the kitchens, through the outer close, and out through the front entrance of the castle.

From the top of the hill, they could see the miniature castle in the valley below. The royal entourage and the diplomats sat to one side, at a safe distance. The rest of the castle folk watched from points all around the valley, some from the esplanade, some in a circle around the small wooden keep, and some, including the other musicians and minstrels, from the rise where Mery was.

The wooden keep currently appeared to be under attack. Soldiers of every type launched assault on the castle. Some were dressed as landsknechts, some as Moors. Soldiers disguised as devils fired a pair of cannons at the structure.

Mery clutched at Tristan, shrieking in mock terror as wild Highlanders dressed in animal skins threw flaming spears and lobbed fireballs at the castle.

The fireworks were loud and startling. Mery jumped as splinters of wooden carts, bits of feathers, and tufts of fur exploded outward from the gunpowder blasts. She could see why the queen had put the prince to bed.

"Won't the soldiers be injured?" she yelled out to Tristan.

"Nae. They're wearin' thick pads."

Even so, from all the scattered debris she saw in the brief flares of firelight, she thought it would be a miracle if no one was hurt.

Of course, the keep withstood it all. The message was clear. Prince James would triumph, no matter what destructive forces arose to challenge him.

That message didn't seem to offend the English. Despite the crack of gunfire, the thunderous explosions, and the searing flashes that lit the sky, even the morose hurdy-gurdy player and the timid lutist were oohing and ahhing over the brilliant spectacle.

Suddenly, as a fireball streaked across the sky, Mery saw it double in her vision. She blinked and shook her head. But when she looked again, it was still blurry. The noises around her seemed to retreat and echo, as if she'd entered a tunnel.

She turned to Tristan. He was saying something. But she couldn't exactly figure out what. She staggered, and he caught her elbow, frowning at her in concern.

"What's wrong?" Tristan asked.

Mery's eyes seemed unfocused. Her brow was dotted with sweat.

"I don't know," she said, her voice rough. "I feel… strange."

As a cook, his first thought was food sickness. What had he served at supper that had disagreed with her?

"Mery?"

"So hot." She gave him a hoarse chuckle. "My voice," she said, touching her throat. "What's wrong with my voice?"

"Mery!" he said in alarm. "What did ye eat?"

She blinked at him in confusion.

"At supper," he said, gripping her by the shoulders, "what did ye eat?"

Her head dropped forward, but she jerked it back up.

"What did ye eat, Mery?"

"Nothin'."

"Nothin'? Are ye sure?"

"So thirsty…" She gulped and touched her throat again.

His heart raced. If she was having trouble swallowing…

"Did ye drink anythin'?"

Her head lolled again.

"Mery!"

"What?"

"What did ye drink?"

"I was thirsty," she rasped out. "I didn't mean to steal it."

"Steal what? What, Mery?"

"The gold cup."

"The gold cup?" What was she talking about? "What gold cup?"

"The wee one."

Tristan narrowed his eyes, trying to think. The prince drank out of a small gold cup. He recalled that the vessel had been brought to the table, but it had somehow been empty. He'd had to fetch George Boag, the man in charge of the prince's beverages, to fill it. "The wee gold cup on the servin' table?"

She nodded. "Sorry."

Suddenly he couldn't draw air into his lungs. "What was in it? What did ye drink, Mery?"

"Watered wine...I think. Didn't mean to..."

Tristan felt the world tilt and tumble as the awful truth reared its horrid head. Someone had poured poison into that cup—poison meant for the prince. In all the confusion, no one had noticed. But the prince hadn't drunk it. Mery had.

He stared at her in horror. What kind of poison was it? Was she going to die?

She gulped again, winced, and reached for her throat. If there was any hope of saving her, he had to move quickly.

His heart pounding painfully against his ribs, he hefted her up in his arms. "Make way!" he bellowed, fighting his way through the packed crowd.

Once free, he bolted across the courtyard toward the kitchens. His mind was racing, trying to determine what poison she could have taken. He clambered down the stairs and started barking out orders to the staff the instant he entered.

"Murray, bring mustard and dill! Wat, a bit of oil! Chris, a pitcher o' fresh water! Hurry!"

He set Mery carefully down on the turnbrochie's stool. She was grimacing, holding her throat, and she kept blinking her eyes. He tipped up her chin to look into her pupils. They were huge. He instantly recognized the sign.

"Dwale."

The deadly plant was rare in Scotland, but plentiful in the south of England. Its sweet flavor made it an undetectable poison. A handful of berries could kill a man. But before death came thirst, dizziness, visions, and enlarged pupils.

The kitchen lads stopped what they were doing. They immediately brought him what he wanted. Leaning Mery back against the corner, he set about grinding the mustard and dill together.

"Watch o'er her," he said to Easson and Campbell. The lads were eager to help. They kept her from falling over, even if Easson's soot-blackened hands left marks on her pristine white gown.

Thomas Chalmers stormed into the room then. Glimpsing Mery, he bellowed, "I thought I told ye—" He broke off when he saw her condition. "What's wrong with ye?" He wheeled toward Tristan. "What's wrong with her?"

"She's been poisoned," he choked out.

"What!" Thomas snapped. "From the kitchens?"

"Nae." At least, he didn't *think* it had come from the kitchens. But if he found out anyone on his staff had slipped dwale into that drink...

Thomas glanced again at Mery, who was drooping against the wall, then whispered, "What kind o' poison?"

"Dwale."

Thomas ran a hand over his chin and nodded to the herbs Tristan was grinding. "Ye'll be emptyin' her belly then."

"Aye."

Just then, Mery stirred. She tried to speak, but no words came out. She ran her tongue slowly over her lips. She was thirsty. That was one of the signs of dwale poisoning.

"Just a moment, darlin'," he called out to her as calmly as he could. "I'll bring ye somethin' to drink."

He added a generous helping of oil to the pitcher of water, and then stirred the mustard and dill into it. It would taste nasty. But hopefully, her thirst would make her drink it anyway. He poured a third of it into a large mazer.

He knelt before her and took hold of her jaw with one trembling hand.

"Here, lass. This will slake your thirst."

He tipped the mazer between her lips. She swallowed once and then, with a grimace of disgust, turned away.

"I know," he said. "It tastes like shite. But ye have to drink it all. Ye've been poisoned, Mery. Ye need to get rid of the poison."

She blinked slowly, trying to understand. "Poison? Ye want me to drink poison?"

"Nae. This isn't poison." He held her chin again. He could force her to drink the stuff. In her weakened state, the turnbrochies could hold her down while he poured it down her throat.

But he knew Mery. The more she was forced, the less likely she was to do a thing. Maybe there was another way.

"Ye know," he said, "the lads here said they don't think ye can drink this down all at once."

Campbell and Easson looked at each other. Of course, they'd said no such thing.

She frowned at the mazer. "That?"

"Aye. It tastes so foul, they say no lass can do it."

She looked doubtfully at the cup, then licked her parched lips. "I can do it."

He helped her with the drink. True to her word—though by her shudder, it must have tasted terrible—she guzzled down every last drop.

"Good lass. Campbell, fetch a basin. She'll be wantin' it soon. And Will, I'll need fresh cream—a pitcher full."

Meanwhile, Tristan would keep her as comfortable as possible...and pray harder for her than he'd ever prayed in his life.

# CHAPTER 22

ery wasn't sure how she'd gotten to the chamber above the kitchens. She was seated on a bench at the table. She was thirsty. The room was too bright. All she wanted was to lie down and go to sleep. But the people crowded around wouldn't let her.

She remembered vomiting into a basin, drinking cream, then more of that wretched-tasting mixture, and vomiting again. Tristan had told her that was good. But how could it be good? She must be sick.

Every few moments, someone offered her a dram of whisky. Yet her throat still felt dry. When she tried to talk, only a croak came out. They spoke to her. She heard their words. But she couldn't make sense of them.

"Come on, lass," Harry said. "Ye can fight this."

The master cook chimed in. "Ye pull through, lassie, and I promise ye can come to the kitchens any time."

"Oh, Mery," Ginny the other soprano wailed. "Ye have to get better. Ye just have to. I can't sing all by myself."

Sing? She wondered if she could sing. She wasn't sure she could speak.

Tristan sat beside her. His arm was wrapped around her shoulders. She closed her eyes and leaned into the crook of his arm. He was so strong and supportive. And she was so tired.

She was about to nod off when Tristan poked her, offering her more whisky.

"Nae," she complained. Why did everyone want to ply her with drink? Couldn't they see she was already soused?

"Come, lass," he murmured, "'twill keep ye awake...and alive."

She took a sip, wishing it were thirst-quenching water instead of throat-burning whisky.

Elspeth the alto was staring closely at her. "Her eyes are as big as shillin's."

Anne the other alto clucked her tongue. "Do ye think she can see us?"

Mery let her eyes drift to the left of them. Some of the musicians were here, speaking nervously in the corner. She wondered what they were worried about.

It didn't matter. She would go to sleep now, and when she woke up...

"Mery!" Tristan patted her cheek, making her scowl in annoyance. "Stay with me!"

She squinted into his face. It was indistinct. But she recognized him. "Tristan."

"Aye."

She was happy he was here. She smiled. At least she thought she smiled. She wasn't sure. She couldn't feel her face.

"Ye have to stay awake," he told her.

She furrowed her brow. There was something she

wanted to ask him. Something important. After the fireworks. What was it?

"Tristan?" Her voice was little more than a harsh whisper.

"Aye?"

"Is it over?"

"Is what over?"

"The fireworks."

"Aye."

She shook her head, trying to disperse the fog. Now she remembered.

"Tristan."

"Aye?"

"Will ye marry me?"

The whole room fell instantly silent. No doubt everyone had heard Mery's question.

Tristan gulped. Could the situation be any worse?

Mery might be dying. She certainly wasn't in her right mind. She might not even know what she was saying.

Everyone knew he wasn't good enough for Mery Graham. Worse, he was still dressed up in his ridiculous satyr costume. How could he answer with any dignity?

Yet what kind of heartless bastard would they think he was if he turned her down? Even if it was for her own good.

Then he looked into her eyes. They were soft with affection. Even under the influence of poison and whisky, it was clear that her heart belonged to him.

Suddenly, he didn't care if theirs was a doomed love. He didn't care if anyone approved. He didn't think about the future. He didn't consider the consequences. He just seized the day.

"Aye," he told her, as sure of his answer as he'd ever been sure of anything. "I will."

Unfortunately, she'd slipped off into sleep.

But to his amazement, the room exploded in cheers, which roused her again. Even Harry seemed overjoyed. He and the master cook clapped each other on the back, as if they'd planned the whole thing.

Easson and Campbell punched each other in the shoulder. The English musicians applauded. Some of the minstrels grinned, and some looked ready to weep, but they all looked glad.

He shook his head in wonder. Then he gazed again at Mery.

Her brow was creased in confusion. "What happened?"

"I said aye."

Now that he'd surrendered, his heart filled with love. He couldn't believe the lovely lass was going to be his. He didn't know how they'd work it all out. But he supposed they'd find a way. He knew, from now on, everything would be all right.

Until she whispered, "Aye?"

Already she'd forgotten. But he knew what was in her heart. So he made her a challenge she couldn't refuse.

"Aye. If ye promise me, Mery Graham, that ye'll stay awake, I'll marry ye."

"Ye will?" Her face lit up.

He nodded.

She blinked, trying to keep her eyes open. Squirming out of his arms, she tried to sit upright. "Ye promise?" she croaked.

"I promise."

Mery stayed true to her end of the bargain. Though it was obviously a great struggle for her, she managed to resist the urge to drift into slumber. The bracing gulps of whisky helped, as did the songs the minstrels performed to keep her entertained.

His only sorrow was that she couldn't sing along. Her voice was but a rough rasp now. Fortunately, under the influence of so much drink, Mery found her own attempts to sing amusing and not tragic. But he wondered if—God willing, she survived—she would ever regain her angelic voice.

He didn't care—not for himself. As far as he was concerned, she could be blind and mute for the rest of her life. He just wanted her to live. But he worried about how she would feel. She might not be able to sing again.

The next hour was hell for Tristan. He never left her side. Now that he'd begun to think of Mery as his bride, he couldn't bear losing her. The thought of letting death snatch her from his arms slashed across his heart like a butcher's knife.

She fought with the determination of a soldier. And yet she seemed to grow no stronger. While he coaxed her on with encouragements, his own soul felt heavy with despair.

"Lad," Thomas said, nudging him with a loaf of barley bread, "ye've got to keep up your own strength."

Tristan nodded, though he didn't feel much like eating. He tore off a piece of bread with his teeth, chewed, and swallowed. But he didn't taste it.

He offered Mery a wee bite. She turned her head away. After three cups of that horrible concoction he'd given her to rid her of the poison, he couldn't blame her for having no appetite.

When the minstrels took a short break from singing, Harry came up, crouching beside Mery. His eyes were red—not from drink, but from weeping. Tristan couldn't blame the man. He'd practically been a father to Mery. No one had more cause for anguish.

"She'll survive, ye know," Harry said to him. "She's a fighter. I've seen her do things...well, no ordinary lass would dare." He took Mery's pale hand and ran his thumb across her knuckles. "Isn't that right, lass?"

"Harry." She smiled weakly, but it was obvious his words weren't sinking in.

A wee sob escaped Harry, but he sniffed back his tears. "Aye, lass, 'tis Harry. Ye get better now. We're countin' on ye." He gave Tristan a meaningful look. "*All* of us."

Tristan suddenly felt like a lump of dough had lodged in his throat. Never had he imagined the leader of the minstrels would allow, much less approve, of a match between their beloved soprano and a lowly cook.

He clasped the man's hand in fellowship. With a nod, Harry stood and returned to lead the minstrels in another song.

Easson and Campbell had been staring in silence for some time. Easson suddenly broke away and rushed up to Tristan, much to the consternation of his older friend.

"Do ye want me to roast somethin' up for her?" he blurted.

Campbell whacked Easson on the back of his head for his impertinence. Easson gave Campbell a shove in return.

Tristan mustered up a smile for the wee lad. Easson

was on the path to being a true cook if he thought every problem could be solved with food.

"I don't think she's of a mind to eat a roast just now, lad. But 'twas kind o' ye to offer."

Easson made a smug face at Campbell, who rolled his eyes.

The English musicians came up in a pack then. They were still wearing their nymph costumes. When Mery saw them, she cocked her head and studied them at length, trying to make sense of the men in flowing, multi-colored gowns.

"Is there anything we can do?" whispered the lutist.

"We'd offer to play," the hurdy-gurdy man growled, "but our instruments were taken back to the spectacle shop."

"How was I to know we'd need them?" the harpist said with a frown. "Besides, 'twas decent of the lad to offer to pack them back to our lodgings so the rest of us could watch the fireworks."

The viol player sighed. "Is there anything *else* we can do?"

Tristan gave them a weak smile. "Pray."

He prayed with the fervency of a saint. He vowed he'd go to church every Sabbath, work harder in the kitchens, give to the poor. He promised he'd look after Mery for the rest of her life, if only God would save her.

# CHAPTER 23

Mery had been awake all along. But now she felt as if she were rousing very slowly from a dream. It took her a long time to remember precisely what had happened. The room was lit by a single candle. She remembered it was because the bright light hurt her eyes. It was hard to see the faces of those around her. But she knew now who they were.

The closest was Tristan, clasping her hand. She was amused to see he was still in his satyr costume. But he looked so very weary. A deep crease divided his brows, and his shoulders were hunched forward as if they bore the weight of the world.

She was thirsty.

She tried to say, "Water," but all that came out was a reedy wisp of air.

Still, it was enough to get Tristan's attention.

"What do ye need?" he asked, as attentive as a loyal hound.

She couldn't speak well, so she touched her throat.

"More whisky?"

She vehemently shook her head. She didn't think she'd ever drink whisky again. It might have kept her awake, but it didn't quench her thirst. In fact, it made it worse.

"Watered wine?"

She nodded.

A serving lad was there with a cup before Tristan could even say a word.

"Thank ye, Campbell."

He gave her the wine. With shaking hands, she lifted it to her mouth and drank. The drink was refreshing after the noxious mixture she'd downed earlier and all the drams of whisky she'd put away. She was starting to feel better already.

"Ye look good," Tristan said hopefully. "How do ye feel?"

She gave him a weak smile.

"I think she's improvin'," he announced to the others.

Everyone came up to see for themselves.

Harry gazed into her eyes. "Can ye see now? Do ye know who we are?"

Not trusting her voice, she gave him a scolding frown and a nod.

"Oh, lass, we were all so worried," he said. "But ye're feelin' better, aye?"

She couldn't make out his features distinctly. But she heard the grief in his voice. He really had been worried about her.

She nodded. She was feeling *much* better. But she still couldn't see well, and she still couldn't speak. What she *could* do—what she desperately wanted to do—was to eat.

"Tristan," she whispered.

"Aye?"

"Food?"

"Ye're hungry?" His eyes lit up. "That's a good sign. What would ye like? I'll make ye whatever ye want."

She might be groggy, but she couldn't resist coaxing a laugh from him. "Bustard."

The musicians chuckled.

Tristan managed a small smile. "I suppose ye want a slice o' the moon with a sprinklin' o' stars on top as well?"

She smiled back.

Everyone fussed over her after that, bringing her food, wrapping a cloak about her, lending her slippers to keep her bare feet warm.

She didn't think she'd been as near death as most of them claimed. At least, it hadn't felt like it. She only seemed to be not quite Mery Graham, like a dream version of herself. Aside from great thirst, her lost voice, and her blurred vision, she felt like her mind was intact.

Then she remembered the promise. Tristan had promised her that if she stayed awake, he would marry her. At least, she hoped that was a promise and not a false memory from that dream state.

She had to find out.

When he came near with a small dish of applemoise, she tugged on his sash. He bent his ear close.

"Marry me?" she whispered.

His face grew very serious. He set aside the applemoise. Then he lowered himself onto one knee, taking her hands in his.

"I will marry ye...if ye'll have me."

"O' course she'll have ye," the master cook boomed. "Ye're a fine catch, MacKenzie."

"Well, now," Harry countered in his equally booming bass, "Mery Graham is not exactly a wee prize."

"Agreed," the master cook said.

"All right then," Harry decided.

The two shook hands.

Mery thought maybe it was a good thing she couldn't speak. She might be tempted to let the two old fools know that she didn't care whether they approved the match or not.

But she was too content to complain. Perhaps it was best to let them believe their opinions mattered.

Mery could feel her strength returning as Tristan and his trusty servers brought her more food. Harry and the master cook compared the virtues of the bride and groom. The minstrels and musicians bolstered her spirits with wedding plans. Before long, she felt almost fully restored.

But one thing was niggling at the back of her mind. What had become of the villain who'd poisoned the wine? What would he do when he discovered his plot had failed? When the prince didn't die, would he try again?

She grabbed Tristan's wrist to get his attention.

"What is it? Are ye all right?"

"The prince," she mouthed.

"Safe and sound."

She shook her head. He might be safe for now, but that could change. "Spy. Caught?"

Tristan straightened. She could tell he was thinking the same thing she had. "He could still be on the loose," he voiced for her. "Once he discovers his plans have been foiled... He may try again."

She nodded.

He let out a decisive breath. "The queen must be warned."


Cooks didn't walk through the royal apartments unless

they'd been summoned. They most definitely didn't stroll into the royals' chambers in breeches made of fur. Tristan had thrown his doublet on, but he hadn't wanted to take the time to change his trews.

After all, he had proof now that there had been an attempt on the prince's life. Time was of the essence. Surely he'd be forgiven his lack of protocol since his bride-to-be had saved the prince's life once already.

The moment he got close to the prince's chambers, he was intercepted by four guards.

"I must speak with the prince's guardian," he told them. "'Tis urgent."

One of the guards gave him a thorough perusal and a disparaging smirk. "Sorry. They don't allow beasts in the prince's chambers."

The others snickered.

Tristan fumed. He felt his cheeks redden. "I'm one o' the castle cooks," he ground out.

"Is that so?" another guard asked, elbowing his giggling companion.

Tristan didn't have time for their amusement. "I need to get a message to the prince's guardian. 'Tis a matter o' life and death."

"Whose life and death?" the first guard asked.

"The prince's."

The guard sobered somewhat and narrowed his eyes. "The prince's?"

"Aye. He's in danger."

"What sort o' danger?"

Tristan explained everything. How Mery had overheard the English ambassador planning to coerce the queen into signing the treaty, no matter the cost. How someone had slipped dwale into the prince's cup at supper. How Mery had consumed it by mistake and was suffering the effects of the poison even now. He said he feared that the culprit, realizing he'd been thwarted, would make a second attempt on the prince's life. It was imperative that the English spy be hunted down and exposed for what he was.

The guard considered his words and finally let out an annoyed sigh. "Fine. But if this comes to nothin', 'twill be a matter o' life and death for *ye.*"

Tristan nodded curtly.

"Wait here," the guard said as he quietly opened the door to the prince's chambers and ducked inside.

Tristan spent several minutes enduring the sniggering mockery of the guards. He entertained himself by imagining the various ingredients he could mix into their pottage at supper the next day—pig shite, bird droppings, goat piss. It was never wise to anger one's cook.

At last the guard emerged, closing the door softly behind him.

"What news?" Tristan asked.

"The prince is sleepin' peacefully. A close watch will be kept o'er him."

"But that's not enough," Tristan said. "The perpetrator must be caught and brought to justice."

"'Tisn't up to me."

"What if he tries again?"

"He'll fail, I suppose."

"Ye *hope.* But what if he doesn't?" Tristan clenched his fists. "What if ye could have stopped him and ye didn't?"

The guard sighed. It was obvious Tristan was right. "Listen," he confided. "The truth of it is the queen wants to maintain diplomacy between the countries. To cast blame on the English at this sensitive time could destroy the fragile peace."

"What?" Tristan was livid. "Ye mean they plan to let him walk free?"

"I told ye, 'tisn't up to me. I'm sorry about the minstrel. But maybe a closer watch should be kept o'er the kitchens if a spy can slip poison into the wine."

Tristan clenched his jaw hard enough to crack a walnut, shell and all. No one had sneaked into his kitchens. And it was an insult for the man to say so. But it would do no good to rile the royal guards. They'd likely toss him out on his furry arse.

Still, he couldn't just stand by and do nothing. With a silent curse, he turned on his heel and strode away.

He'd always liked the queen. She was wise and energetic, kind and generous. But he supposed, like all royals, she believed the lives of nobles were more valuable than those of commoners. Her son hadn't been poisoned, so it was of little consequence to her what happened to the villain who had failed to poison him.

But it was hard for Tristan to see things that way.

He'd almost lost Mery. It choked him up just to think about it. And maybe she hadn't died. But she'd suffered for hours. She was half-blind. Her voice had been ruined. She might never get it back.

Somebody needed to pay. And if the queen wasn't going to pursue the culprit, he would.

All the way back to the kitchens, he considered who could have had access and opportunity.

It had to have been done in the short interval between the time the cup of wine left the kitchens and when Mery drank it, right before the last course.

He knew nobody in the kitchens was responsible. They were all faithful servants, loyal to the queen. Tristan had known most of them for years, and he'd trust them with his life. And, with the exception of Mery, no stranger ever entered the kitchens.

Because of the stage collapse, Tristan himself had directed the servants in reseating the guests. That was just before the table with the cup had been rolled out by four servers.

So who could have poisoned the wine?

There had been a number of actors cavorting about the great hall. But after the chaos of the collapse, Pagez had kept them out of the way at the far end of the chamber.

Once the table was rolled out, the only people who would have been close enough to access the gold cup were the minstrels and musicians.

He couldn't imagine it was one of them. They'd stood by Mery's side through her ordeal. Aye, the consort was English. But as musicians, they'd shown a brotherly devotion to her that stretched beyond borders.

Still, when he finally arrived back in the room where Mery was, he eyed everyone there with new suspicion.

"Did ye warn the queen?" Thomas asked him.

"Aye."

"Good." Thomas clapped the matter from his hands. "I'll be down in the roastin' room then. No doubt the castle is goin' to want a big feast on the morrow to prepare for the manhunt." He made his exit and tromped down the stairs.

Tristan's heart sank. Manhunt. There would be no manhunt. As long as the prince was safe, no one cared if the man who'd hurt Mery came to justice.

His gaze drifted over to her. The color had returned to

her cheeks. The other lady minstrels were fawning over her, making grand plans for the wedding to come.

He still couldn't believe he'd agreed to such an impulsive act. But he wasn't sorry. Mery was going to make the most perfect wife. And he was going to try his best to make her a good husband.

Starting with finding and punishing the arse-wisp of a villain who had dared to hurt her.

He glanced about the chamber again. What had he overlooked? Who had the face of a murderer?

All at once, he realized someone was missing.

# CHAPTER 24

He couldn't tell Mery he was leaving. She'd insist on coming along, no matter the danger and no matter how incapacitated she was. So he had to slip out unnoticed.

While the others were helping themselves to the whisky, he made his escape to the kitchens. He quickly changed into his shirt, doublet, and trews, then threw a cloak over his shoulders.

"Where are ye goin'?" Thomas asked.

Tristan hesitated. He couldn't hide anything from Thomas. He grabbed up a butcher's knife from the block. "Huntin'."

Thomas's eyes widened, and he came close so the kitchen lads couldn't hear. "Now hold on, lad. Ye aren't goin' to do anythin' foolish, are ye?"

Tristan compressed his lips in answer and tried to pass Thomas.

Thomas blocked him, hissing, "Wait till the morrow, lad. Don't try to do anythin' by yourself. Let the queen's men—"

"The queen's men aren't interested," he bit out. "As long

as the prince is safe, 'tis no matter to them if the culprit is ever found."

"Ye don't know that."

"I do. They told me themselves." He pushed past Thomas then.

"MacKenzie!"

Tristan froze. After all these years, it was second nature to respond to the master cook's bark.

Thomas growled, "Ye come back safe, do ye hear me? I've spent too many years trainin' ye to have ye murdered in some dark alley."

Tristan knew that was as close to condoning his actions yet expressing his concern as Thomas could manage. He gave the master cook a nod of reassurance and then swept out the door and into the night.

The fireworks were over. But as Tristan hurried down the esplanade, he saw the soldiers were still awake, cleaning the armaments and putting out stray sparks.

Pungent smoke hung in the air, and the green was littered with broken arrows, blackened spears, and spent fireballs. Wooden fragments of the destroyed castle—from gigantic exploded planks to long and deadly slivers—were everywhere. It would take days to restore the field.

In the dark and amid the chaos, Tristan realized the one he hunted could be hiding anywhere. But the first place he'd look was where the man claimed to have gone—to their lodgings to return the instruments.

Tristan knew the owners of the spectacle shop. They were a kind couple. The man was an old soldier with a mechanical leg. His wife made the spectacles. There were children in the house. Tristan didn't want anything bad to happen to them. But it might be worse to leave them alone with an English spy.

He concealed his knife when Lachlan Mar answered the door.

"MacKenzie. Welcome." He let Tristan in.

"Mar. Good evenin'."

"Come on up. Alisoune will be glad to see ye. She's been chatterin' on about the fireworks for an hour now."

They mounted the steps to the main floor of the house. It never ceased to amaze Tristan how well Lachlan could walk on his mechanical leg. Mar's wife, Alisoune, was sitting at the hearth with three of her children.

"Did ye see the fireworks?" she asked, her eyes aglow behind her spectacles. "The Chinese invented them, ye know, out o' sulfur, charcoal, and saltpe—"

"Darlin'," Lachlan interrupted, "I'm certain MacKenzie didn't come for a lecture on fireworks."

"Sorry," she said with a grin of apology.

"They *were* impressive," Tristan agreed. "But Lachlan's right. I've come about a different matter. Can ye tell me, did any o' the musicians return yet?"

"Aye," Lachlan volunteered. "One o' them brought back an armload o' musical instruments."

Tristan's heart skipped a beat. "And is he still here?"

"Aye," Alisoune replied. "Upstairs."

"May I?" Tristan asked.

"Go on," Lachlan said.

Tristan took a deep, bracing breath and headed up the steps.

When he first opened the door, the tambor player was facing away in the candlelit room, bent over a satchel, stuffing it with clothing.

"Back so soon, darlings?" he sang out. "How were the fireworks?"

Tristan shut the door behind him. "Ye should have been there to see them."

At the sound of Tristan's unfamiliar voice, the tambor player popped up and whirled around.

"Oh! La! You gave me quite a fright." He patted his chest, catching his breath. "The cook, right?"

Tristan didn't answer. His eyes burned as he stared at the man who had poisoned Mery.

For a moment, the man looked uncertain. Then he let his gaze course down and up the length of Tristan's body, then languidly dipped his eyelids. "And, if I recall, a quite handsome satyr."

Tristan ignored the comment. "I'm afraid your plans have gone awry."

"My plans?" The tambor player clasped his hands under his chin and gave Tristan a coy smile. "Pray tell, what plans are those?"

"Your plans to kill the prince."

The tambor player's flinch was almost imperceptible. Nonetheless, it was there. He covered it with a chuckle. "Don't be ridic—"

"He's alive and well," Tristan said.

"Well, that's good news," the man said lightly. "'Twould be a shame to have gone to the trouble of a three-day banquet if he weren't." He lowered his eyes and picked a piece of lint off of his doublet. "Though I fail to see what that has to do with m—"

"The poison was drunk by someone else."

"Poison?" The man clapped a palm to his cheek in false shock. "What poison?"

Tristan skewered the villain with a glare. "Ye almost killed the woman I love," he bit out. He drew his butcher's knife slowly from his doublet. The tambor player's eyes widened. "I should carve ye to bits for the pain ye made her suffer."

The tambor player's gaze darted about as if he were considering his options.

Tristan spun the large blade through his fingers and caught it again by the handle.

The tambor player gulped.

"But I won't," Tristan said. "I'm goin' to leave that up to the authorities." While the queen might not expend any efforts tracking down the man who'd tried to poison her son, Tristan was certain if he delivered the villain into her hands, she'd have no choice but to make an example of him.

The tambor player straightened then, dropping his effeminate affectations. His voice lowered. His lisp was gone. "You have no proof. Your threats are empty."

"If that's so, then how do ye think I found ye?"

The man's mouth worked as his eyes flitted about in desperation. He was trapped, and he knew it.

Suddenly, the tambor player snatched the candle out of its sconce. Holding it before him like a weapon, he dug something out of his satchel. It looked like a ball made out of paper with a string coming out of it.

Tristan narrowed his gaze. He recognized what the man held. He'd seen crates of them on the boats that had brought fireworks from Edinburgh.

The tambor player held the flame close to the string and snarled, "There's enough explosive in this to kill both of us. I'm willing to sacrifice my life for the queen, the *true* queen, Elizabeth. How about you? Are you willing to die for her pretender cousin?"

Tristan froze. If Mery had died, he might have gladly let himself be blown up if it meant taking her killer with him. But she hadn't died. He had something to live for.

From the doorway came a quick gasp. One of Lachlan's children must have heard their voices and come up the stairs. "Is that a petard?" she asked in tones of hushed awe.

Tristan grimaced. He hid his knife inside his doublet. The last thing he wanted to do was to get the innocent Mar family involved in a dangerous situation.

"Copernica!" her mother called from downstairs. "Leave the men alone."

"Mama, they have a petard!"

Tristan stiffened. No doubt Alisoune Mar was already halfway up the steps.

"A what?" she yelled back.

"Ye know, Mama," the wee lass continued, "like the ones they had at the fireworks!"

Bloody hell, this was going from bad to worse. He looked with grim entreaty at the tambor player, shaking his head, wordlessly begging the man not to light the bomb.

He'd hoped the villain would tuck it away again, his point made. The man couldn't be so ruthless as to kill an innocent child in cold blood, could he?

But then he remembered this was the same monster who'd tried to poison an infant.

Unfortunately, the tambor player had no intention of losing his leverage. And when Alisoune showed up a moment later with a gasp that was an echo of her daughter's, he reacted with cold calculation.

"We're all going to walk down the stairs now," the man said, shouldering his satchel, "calmly, quietly. No one will say anything. You'll bid me a fond farewell, and I'll make my way safely out of your stinking Scottish city. Or...I can light this."

# CHAPTER 25

espite the wonderful company and delicious food, Mery was growing weary. The poison had taken more out of her than she realized.

But she knew it was the musicians' and minstrels' last night together. They wanted to make the most of it. She wondered if Tristan would accompany her back to their lodgings so she could get some sleep.

She tried to see in the dim light. Where was Tristan?

She tugged at Anne's sleeve and whispered, "Have ye seen Tristan?"

Anne shook her head.

"Harry," she called roughly across the room.

He came to her side. "What is it?"

"Have ye seen Tristan?"

"Not since he came back from the prince's chamber."

She frowned. Maybe he was downstairs in the kitchens, fixing her some special dish.

"Campbell," she rasped. He couldn't hear her. "Campbell," she tried again. He was oblivious. "Easson."

That name the lad heard at once and came to her with a wee bow. "Aye, my lady?"

"Where is MacKenzie?"

"I don't know, my lady. He left the kitchens about an hour ago and—"

"An hour?"

A cold lump lodged in Mery's throat. Where had he gone? She leaned back against the wall, stunned.

"Are ye all right, Mery?" Ginny asked.

"He's gone." She felt numb.

"Who's gone?"

"Tristan."

"What do ye mean, 'gone'?"

"He's not comin' back."

"Ye don't know that," Elspeth chimed in. "He's probably just gone to take a piss or somethin'."

Mery shook her head. He'd been gone too long for that.

"He ran off." Her heart sank as she realized the truth. "He didn't want to marry me."

"Ballocks!" Ginny said. "Who wouldn't want to marry ye?"

Mery began thinking about all the times they'd been together, all the times she'd said she loved him.

But he'd never said it in return. Not once.

Maybe he didn't love her. And maybe he was too ashamed to tell her so. Instead, he'd taken the coward's way out. He'd run off.

Anne decided to take matters into her own hands. "Where's MacKenzie?" she demanded. "Where has he gone? Speak up, lads!"

Mery felt a hollow caving in her chest where her heart used to be. Tristan wasn't coming back. Not ever. He'd stayed with her when she was at death's door. But the moment she didn't need him anymore, he'd left.

Harry was the first to reply. "He's gone?" He shook his head, disappointed, then rubbed a palm across his chin, wondering what to say. "Look, lass," he told her, "ye know the minstrels will always be here for ye...as long as, God willin', your voice returns."

Mery's eyes filled with tears. What if her voice didn't return? What if her vision didn't return? Was she doomed to an existence without a trade and without a husband? Would she have to return to Nairn and become a fisherman's wife?

Seeing Mery's crestfallen expression, Harry clenched and unclenched his hands in frustration. "I have half a mind to... Let me speak to his master."

Mery doubted it would do any good. Besides, she didn't want a husband who'd been compelled to wed her at the point of a sword. She wanted him to come to her of his own free will.

But before she could explain that, Harry was off down the stairs.

When he returned, it was with Thomas Chalmers in tow. The master cook looked cross, as if he were being dragged in front of a judge.

Harry spoke. "Tell her what ye told me."

Thomas wrenched his arm out of Harry's grip. "He's comin' back, lass. He only went to...take care of an urgent affair."

"What urgent affair?" Mery said on a wheeze.

He hesitated.

Harry elbowed him.

"Fine," he said, scowling at Harry. Then he sighed and

confessed to her, "He's lookin' for the man who did this to ye."

"What?" Mery was filled simultaneously with relief and dread.

"He's a cautious man, but…" The master cook shook his head. "But the look in his eye…"

"Where did he go?" she asked.

"He didn't say. He…he took a knife and left."

The women gasped.

Mery's brow creased. "A knife?"

They all began talking at once. But Mery wasn't listening. All she could think was that the man she loved was out there alone, facing a trained killer…with a kitchen knife.

As he watched the tambor player make his way down the dark streets of Stirling, it took all of Tristan's willpower not to hurl the butcher's knife into the fleeing villain's back.

It was Alisoune who stayed his arm. "Nae!" she hissed. "Ye can't risk an explosion in the middle o' Stirlin'. Some petards are so powerful, they can flatten a stone wall."

"Then I'll follow him till he's out o' town," Tristan bit out.

She tightened her grip on his arm. "'Tisn't worth it, lad. He said he was leavin' Stirlin', aye?"

"I'd rather he didn't make it," Tristan snarled.

"I can see that. But tell me, is whatever ye're hopin' to gain by killin' him worth riskin' your life?"

He raised his chin in challenge. "Maybe."

She stared at him through her spectacles, as if she was

measuring his mettle. "Fine then," she said, letting go of his arm. "I'll just get my husband to go with ye so ye don't—"

"What?" he whispered. "Nae!"

She crossed her arms and arched a slender brow. "Ye don't know the first thing about fightin', Tristan MacKenzie. But my husband was a soldier. So if ye're goin' to be so foolish as to go after a man with a petard, ye'd best go with someone who knows what he's doin'."

"Nae!"

"'Tisn't like I'll be able to stop Lachlan once he finds out."

"He doesn't have to find out."

"He always finds out."

Tristan's mouth worked in frustration. There was no way he was going to endanger one-legged Lachlan Mar. And he could see by Alisoune's cheeky expression that she knew that.

He muttered a curse under his breath.

Lachlan always said his wife was a clever lass. Fiendishly clever.

Tristan supposed she was also right. The English spy probably wasn't worth pursuing. He'd failed in his mission. He wouldn't get a chance to try again. The danger was past. The prince was safe. And Mery was alive.

Nonetheless, he watched the villain until he was out of sight to be sure he was headed out of town and away from the castle. Then, with a sigh, he let Alisoune invite him back upstairs for a soothing cup of mulled wine.

When Lachlan saw the resigned expression on Tristan's face, he frowned. "What was that all about?"

Alisoune handed her husband a cup of wine.

"Da!" Copernica said, her eyes round. "The man had a petard!"

"Ye said that before, lassie," Lachlan said, giving her a patronizing pat on the head. Then he turned to Alisoune. "Ye shouldn't have filled her wee head with fireworks. We'll ne'er hear the end of it. So what's the real story?" He took a drink of wine.

Behind her spectacles, Alisoune lifted a brow. "The man had a petard."

Lachlan nearly spit his wine. "Ye're jestin', right?"

She shook her head.

Lachlan shot to his feet. "Why didn't ye call me?"

Tristan caught a smug glance from Alisoune that said she'd told him so.

He started to reply. "He said if we didn't keep quiet, he'd..." Then he glanced at wee Copernica. He didn't want to scare the lass.

Lachlan clenched his jaw. "Where is he?" He strode to the fireplace and hefted up a great broadsword.

"Gone, Lachlan," Alisoune told him, resting a soothing hand on his tense forearm. "And 'tis for the best."

Tristan told them the story then of how the villain had meant to poison the prince, how Mery had been poisoned instead, and how, for the sake of keeping the peace, the royals didn't intend to bring him to justice.

Now, neither could he.

Lachlan nodded. "When ye get to be my age, lad, ye'll learn that sometimes justice comes at too great a price." He wrapped an arm around Alisoune's waist. "'Tis better to let it go and be grateful for what ye have."

Tristan knew he was probably right. Lachlan and Alisoune had each other. They had a fine home, lots of children, even a grandchild on the way. He should be glad that Mery was alive so they could have a chance at such contentment.

"But if ye ever need my blade," Lachlan added, "I'll be there in a heartbeat."

Tristan thanked him. It was no light offer. In spite of his mechanical leg, Lachlan was an expert swordsman who had taught many of the lads of Stirling how to fight.

Just before he left, Alisoune stopped him at the shop door.

"The poison was dwale, ye say?"

"Aye."

"So her eyes will be botherin' her?"

"Aye."

"I have just the thing." She rummaged through a box of spectacles and withdrew a pair with darkened lenses. "These are made o' smoky quartz. They'll help to block out the light."

With a smile of thanks, he swore the Mars to silence on the matter and left the shop. As he trudged back up the esplanade, he wondered what lie he was going to tell Mery.

# CHAPTER 26

aiting was killing Mery. She had to go after Tristan. Never mind that she was still recovering from poison. Never mind that she was half-blind, mostly mute, and a wee woman with no combat experience. She couldn't bear the idea that he was out there by himself—a cook on the trail of a skilled assassin.

Harry would never allow her to do something so risky. So she'd have to sneak out under his nose.

Claiming she had to use the garderobe, she stole off. She snatched a cloak that was left on a peg by the door and escaped into the night.

The long walk in the cold air took more out of her than she cared to admit. As she left the castle, she stopped to catch her breath. Below, the valley was littered with fragments of the miniature keep. It was amazing to her— the destructive force of the fireworks. Even more amazing was the fact that the English spy had chosen poison when so many more effective weapons were available.

But then he was a spy. His methods would be

clandestine, not explosive. Which made her worry all the more about Tristan.

Tristan might do well in a fair fight. He certainly had the muscle for it. And she'd seen him handle a blade with dexterity.

But this wouldn't be a fair fight. A villain who would poison a child had no honor, no morality. He'd sooner slip an awl between a man's ribs or push him from a high window than engage in a battle he might lose.

Summoning up what little energy she had left, she continued down the esplanade. She wasn't sure what she'd do when she found him. But she didn't intend to let her husband-to-be face a demon alone.

She was halfway between the castle and the area where the buildings of the town began when she began to feel faint. She stopped in her tracks. The world continued spinning. The stars overhead, peeping between the clouds, blurred and doubled. And then shadows advanced at the edges of her vision.

Dizzy and afraid she might pitch forward and hit her head, she plopped onto her bottom instead in the middle of the road. The white petals of her gown drifted around her like a spent blossom. She sat for a few moments, blinking back the encroaching darkness.

And then she saw a figure coming up the hill.

He looked up. He must have seen her too, for he stopped.

"Mery?" he called out.

"Tristan," she barely breathed.

He burst up the hill, covering the distance between them, and scooped her up from the ground. "Mery, what are ye doin' out here? Ye shouldn't be...'tis cold and...oh, Mery." He set her on her feet and hugged her to his chest.

A rush of emotions filled her then, so powerful that she couldn't speak for a moment. Her eyes welled with tears, and her throat ached with the need to sob.

But she also longed to punch Tristan in his reckless, irresponsible, adorable face.

Angry at the torment he'd made her endure, she pushed out of his arms, giving him a backwards shove.

"What was that for?" he asked.

She didn't have the words to explain, even if she'd had a voice.

She was overjoyed that he'd returned, safe and sound.

But she was furious with him for leaving in the first place.

Her heart swelled with gratitude.

Her blood boiled with rage.

Sniffing back tears of relief, she pounded on his chest once, twice.

He caught her wrists and looked at her, perplexed. "What's wrong?"

"Ye left me!" she hissed.

"I was comin' back."

"How was I to know that?"

"I wouldn't leave ye, Mery."

"Why didn't ye tell me?"

"Because ye would have insisted on goin' with me."

She took a breath and then couldn't think of what to say. "I...might not have."

He raised a brow. "Oh, aye, ye would. Look at ye. Ye're half dead from poison. Yet ye're out here in the middle o' the night in the dead o' winter. Are ye afraid o' nothin', Mery Graham?"

Chastened, she let her shoulders dropped. "I'm afraid o' losin' ye."

He gave her a smile of sympathy. "Ye're not goin' to lose me."

"I thought ye'd gone. I thought ye didn't want to marry me."

He folded her in his arms again and murmured against her hair. "How could ye think that, lass? I love ye more than anythin'. And I want ye to be my wife. I made ye a promise."

She wept softly then against his chest.

All would be well now.

She might not get her voice back. She might ever not see well again. But she had Tristan.

Then she remembered. She pushed back to look into his face. "What happened to the villain? Did ye find him?"

He tensed his jaw. "Let's go back to the castle. I should tell everyone what's happened."

Mery didn't want to wait. But for now, everything felt right with the world.

She hadn't died from the poison. In fact, her mistake had actually saved the prince's life. Tristan was safe now. And they were going to be married.

She slipped her hand into his, and they made their way slowly up the hill.

Tristan had to carry her the last hundred yards. She was too weak to stand. And to be honest, she was content being held against his heart. So she didn't argue with him when he swept her off her feet.

When they first entered the chamber above the kitchens, to their surprise, it was filled with so much shouting and turmoil that no one noticed them.

Harry was roaring at the master cook in his deep bass voice, blaming him for Mery's disappearance. The master cook matched him, bellow for bellow, alleging that Harry encouraged Tristan to leave. The minstrels and consort were arguing among themselves, hurling accusations and shoving one another. Mery had never seen such disharmony among musicians.

When Tristan set Mery on her feet and slammed the door behind them, everyone silenced with a start.

"What's goin' on here?" Tristan asked.

They all erupted into shouts. Some cheered at their arrival. Some scolded them for their departure. Some slapped their backs. Some shook their fists. Eventually, Tristan managed to quiet everyone.

"What happened, lad?" the master cook asked.

"Before I tell ye," he said, patting his doublet and pulling a pair of spectacles out of it, "Mery, these are a gift from Alisoune Mar." He handed Mery the curious spectacles. They were made with some sort of darkened glass. He helped her place them on her face.

Immediately, she felt relief. She could now look around without squinting.

"Well?" Harry urged.

He sighed. "I know who tried to poison the prince."

"Good!" the harpist said. "Who?"

Ill at ease, Tristan rubbed a hand over the back of his neck. "Ye won't be pleased."

The lutist's brows shot up. "'Twasn't the Earl?"

"Nae." Tristan lowered his gaze to the floor and took a deep breath. "The only ones there at the right time and place..." he said, glancing up at the musicians, "were ye."

Everyone gasped.

"Us?" the hurdy-gurdy player barked. "That's absurd!

We wouldn't poison anyone! In fact, we've been watching over the lass all this time. Why would we—"

"The tambor player," the violist said.

There was silence as they realized he was the only musician not present.

"What?" the harpist burst out.

"Impossible!" the hurdy-gurdy player decided. "That milksop? He couldn't hurt a flea."

The harpist barked out a laugh. "Surely you jest."

"I don't think he's jesting," the lutist murmured.

Mery had to agree that the tambor player was a most unlikely villain. But then she supposed that being unlikely was what made a spy effective.

"Then again...now that I think about it..." the harpist said. "Did any of us know him that well? He's only been with the consort a short while."

The hurdy-gurdy player muttered, "I never liked him."

The lutist shook his head in disbelief. "A spy...in our midst."

"Maybe that's why he offered to take our instruments back," the harpist said. "He was planning to make his escape."

"Our instruments!" the hurdy-gurdy player cried. "Has he taken them?"

"Nae," Tristan said, "they're safe."

"And what about the tambor player?" Harry asked.

Tristan's jaw tensed. "Gone."

"What do you mean, gone?" the hurdy-gurdy player demanded.

Mery saw the muscles in Tristan's jaw working. "I alerted the guards to his whereabouts. By the time I got there, I'm sure he was...dispatched."

The room fell silent.

"He's dead?" the lutist finally whispered.

Tristan nodded, rubbing a knuckle across his lips.

Mery narrowed her eyes at him. She might not be able to see well, but she could tell at once he was lying.

The harpist grimaced. "What will they do with...the body?"

Tristan swallowed.

Mery frowned.

He cleared his throat. "I don't know. The queen doesn't wish to destroy the peace between our countries. I'm sure ye understand."

The harpist gave a toneless whistle.

Tristan eyed the musicians, one by one. "This whole incident is to remain a secret. I trust I have your word on that?"

They readily agreed.

"I still can't believe it." The lutist shook his head. "He seemed so harmless. How could...how could a *musician* do such a thing?"

"I hope you won't hold it against the rest of us," the violist said to Mery.

Mery was quick to reassure them all as best she could. After all, the hurdy-gurdy player was right. They'd stayed by her side, as worried over her welfare as her minstrel companions.

Harry cleared his throat. "Well, if that's settled, I suggest we all go back to our lodgin's and get a good night's rest. We've had a long day, and we'll be leavin' early on the morrow."

Mery's breath caught. She'd forgotten they were leaving so soon. There was a performance at Dalhousie Castle in five days.

Not that it mattered. She could hardly speak. She definitely couldn't sing. Harry would have to find a new soprano.

Perhaps a hasty farewell was best. If they left quickly, there would be no time for lingering goodbyes, no tears, no regrets.

She couldn't deny that her throat ached at the thought of leaving her second family. The idea of never being able to sing again was heartbreaking. She didn't know if she'd ever regain her strength, and she wondered if she'd have to wear dark spectacles forever.

But there was no point wallowing in her misfortune. At least she'd survived.

Shaking off her grim thoughts, she mustered up a smile for the man she was going to marry, the father of her future children, the one with whom she intended to spend the rest of her life.

But the smile he gave her in return was strained and evasive.

A tiny furrow creased her forehead. Again, she sensed that he wasn't being completely honest about what had happened. What had he left unsaid? What was he hiding?

The master cook grumbled at Tristan. "Ye might as well go along with them, MacKenzie. I can see ye won't get any sleep in the kitchens with your ladylove so far away."

"But I can't leave ye alone to—"

"Ach! Ye'll be leavin' me alone soon enough, I wager," the cook groused. But he winked at Tristan before he wheeled and headed down the stairs to the roasting room. "Don't be late for breakfast!"

As the entourage prepared to leave, Mery caught Tristan's arm. "Are ye all right?"

His eyes slid sideways for an instant, just enough to betray his deceit. But then he took both her hands and gazed directly at her. "I am now."

Her smile wavered. He was keeping a secret. What could it be?

Halfway down the esplanade to the spectacle shop, it hit her.

The guards hadn't killed the tambor player.

Tristan had.

# CHAPTER 27

ery shuddered.

Was Tristan a murderer?

The thought was horrifying.

But he'd been very upset about the poison. And he'd taken a knife with him.

Maybe the guards hadn't been there at all. Maybe he'd stabbed the villain himself and dragged him into the forest for the wolves.

She gulped.

She wondered if she'd made a mistake.

She'd always been impulsive. She'd always relied on her instincts. Her heart had told her to marry Tristan.

But maybe she'd been wrong this time.

After all, she didn't know him—not really. He could be short-tempered and quick to violence. Faith, this might not even be his first murder.

On the other hand, he'd killed the man out of loyalty to her.

He'd said the queen didn't want the story of the assassination attempt to see the light of day. There probably had been no royal guards there at all.

So he had taken the matter into his own hands. He'd sought revenge on the villain who'd poisoned the woman he loved. He'd seen justice done.

Which meant they needed to leave Stirling as soon as possible. Every moment they lingered increased the chance that Tristan might be found out.

Gazing into his adoring face as they arrived at the spectacle shop, she realized she couldn't stop loving him, no matter what he'd done. She couldn't imagine being wed to anyone else.

When Alisoune Mar answered the door, Mery thanked her for the dark spectacles.

Alisoune welcomed everyone in and said she had just the thing for Mery's throat. If the woman noticed that the tambor player was missing from the houseguests, she never said a word. And since there was no evidence of a ghastly murder anywhere in the house, Mery guessed Tristan had intercepted the villain somewhere on the streets of Stirling.

The rest of the musicians and minstrels went to bed. Even Tristan retired after giving her a sweet goodnight kiss. She couldn't blame him. He'd had a long and wearying day—managing the kitchens, portraying a satyr, snatching his bride from the jaws of death, taking vengeance on a spy.

Meanwhile, Alisoune fixed Mery a warm caudle of watered wine with ginger, honey, and lemon. She sat with Mery while she drank it and seemed very keen to hear about all of Mery's symptoms.

Finally, her curiosity satisfied, Alisoune spoke of other things.

"Ye haven't known Tristan very long," she said, pushing the spectacles up on her nose.

Mery shook her head.

"But ye're sure he's the one?"

She nodded.

Alisoune smiled. "'Twas that way with my Lachlan." She leaned forward to pat Mery's knee. "Don't fret about the wee things. When 'tis true love, ye muddle through the rest."

Mery smiled. The Mars had certainly muddled through well enough. They had a happy marriage and a whole flock of children to prove it.

She supposed Tristan's secret could be considered a wee thing. She just hoped it was his one and only secret.

Tristan rose early. He needed to get back to the castle to help Thomas with breakfast. But the rest of the entourage was already up. He trudged down the stairs to find them gathered, packed, and ready to depart. Mery was there as well, looking radiant, even in her dark spectacles.

He felt a sudden twinge in his heart.

What if Mery's voice had returned? What if she'd changed her mind? Would it be too hard for her to leave her life as a wandering minstrel? She took so much joy in singing. He couldn't imagine her giving up something she loved so much.

While Lachlan tended the fire, Alisoune was handing out loaves of bread to the travelers. The children were sleeping.

Harry sighed. "Still nothin'?" he asked Mery.

Mery touched her throat and shook her head.

Tristan let out his breath. He couldn't help but feel relieved. It wasn't that he wished Mery ill. He just couldn't bear the thought of losing her.

She bade the minstrels a teary adieu as they journeyed down the road with the packhorse less than an hour later. As they disappeared around the bend, she gave them a final wave.

Tristan came up behind her then and placed his hands gently on her shoulders. "I'm so sorry about your voice."

"My voice?" she said quite clearly.

He wheeled her around to face him. "Your voice! 'Tis back. But ye said ye…"

She gave him a sly grin.

"Ye lied?" he asked in awe.

She shrugged.

"But what about Harry? What about the minstrels?"

"I'm done with the road," she told him with a wide smile. "'Tis time for my next adventure."

He smiled back. But then he reconsidered her words. What if that was all he was to her—another adventure? If so, would she stay around longer than a year or two? Mery was the most impulsive lass he'd ever met. What if, in a few months, she decided to seize the day with someone else?

He was on the path to driving himself mad with doubt until Lachlan stepped forward.

"Look, ye two," he declared sternly. "If ye're goin' to sleep together under this roof tonight, I'm goin' to insist ye have a handfastin' right now."

"A handfastin'?" Mery pressed a hand to her bosom.

"Lachlan!" Alisoune chided.

After all, handfastings were archaic. Most people had proper church weddings now.

Tristan frowned and scratched his chin thoughtfully. "Nae, he's right."

Lachlan gave him a secret wink.

Tristan returned the gesture with a subtle nod of his head. Lachlan had come to his rescue. If he was handfasted to Mery, by tradition, she'd have to stay with him for a year and a day before the marriage was deemed official. By then, he'd know if she intended to be true to him.

"Mery?" Alisoune asked.

"Why not?" She grinned. "The sooner, the better."

Lachlan called out for his children. Half a dozen Mars, most of them bespectacled, straggled down the stairs in their nightclothes.

So it happened that the Mar family served as witnesses to their handfasting. The children looked on in awe. Their mother wrapped one of her hair ribbons around the couple's clasped right hands, binding them loosely together.

Then they spoke their brief vows, pledging themselves to one another until death.

It seemed it was over in a flash. But now they had a year and a day to be certain this was what both of them wanted.

Tristan gave his bride an adoring kiss—as adoring as he could with a half dozen curious young faces gazing upon him. And then, leaving Mery to the care of the Mars for the day, he went to supervise the kitchens for the final time.

A dozen cooks were already stirring and chopping, beating and simmering, slicing and spicing, preparing yet another in a series of endless meals for the nobles.

Tristan sighed as he realized he was tired of cooking for royals. He seldom received praise for his good work, except from the master cook. Indeed, if he was remembered at all for this magnificent banquet, it would doubtless be for his role as a satyr wielding a whip.

Worse, if he advanced to the role of the prince's cook, he'd be stuck preparing plain boiled capons and bread for a wee lad with no teeth.

He wanted something more. He wanted to have his own kitchens and his own staff. And he wanted to prepare food for people who truly relished it.

Maybe it was a foolish dream. But Mery's "seize the day" kept popping into his head. If ever there was a time to be rash, it was now.

He glanced toward the fire. Wee Easson's head kept drooping as he sat on the turnbrochie's stool. Campbell, slouched on his own stool, would have scolded the lad, but he too kept drifting off. Tristan chuckled and let them be. They'd earned a nap after the help they'd given him last night.

Thomas came in just then, yelling over his shoulder loud enough to wake the lads. "And don't crack the eggs this time, Sinclair, or I'll crack your skull!"

Tristan smirked.

"MacKenzie, have ye eaten yet?"

He shook his head.

Thomas dipped into the bakery and stole a hot loaf from the shelf, shuffling it from hand to hand. "Here." He handed it to Tristan. "Come with me, lad."

Tristan chewed on the warm crust as he followed Thomas into the confectionary, where they could be alone.

He wiped his hands on his apron. "Ye love her, don't ye?"

There was no need to ask whom he meant. "Aye."

Thomas gave him a critical eye. "And I assume ye're plannin' to do the right thing?"

He grinned. "Already have. We were handfasted just this morn."

He nodded. "Good." He took a breath that made his chest expand like a bellows, then let it out. "Well, no need to mince words. Here's the crux o' the matter. Ye may have pulled the wool o'er the eyes o' those musicians last night, lad. But I know better."

Tristan frowned. "What are ye—"

"Let me finish," Thomas warned. "Last night ye told me the royals weren't interested in the English spy. They wanted to keep the whole matter a secret. That's why ye set out to find him yourself."

Tristan could already see where this was heading.

"Then ye returned, tellin' everyone the guards killed him. So I'm sayin' to myself, why would the guards follow a cook to town to dispatch a spy they claimed they weren't interested in?"

Tristan lowered guilty eyes.

Thomas leaned forward and confided, "Listen, I don't care if ye sliced the bastard to ribbons with that knife and left him to the crows. But someone's goin' to find out, mark my words. And when that happens, there won't be a damned thing any of us can do to save ye."

# CHAPTER 28

Tristan's jaw dropped. The cook thought he killed the spy himself? He started to deny the charge.

"Ah-ah-ah," Thomas said, silencing him with an upraised palm. "I don't want to know." He sniffed. "Look. Ye've got brilliant skills now. Ye're my best cook. And I know ye don't really want to be cookin' for a bairn for the next five years. So..." He took another bracing breath. "I think, under the circumstances, for your own safety, 'twould be best if ye moved on. Go somewhere else, somewhere far away."

Tristan was stunned. Go away? Thomas couldn't mean that.

His first instinct was to argue with the master cook. He hadn't killed anyone, after all. How could Thomas, who'd been like a father to him, kick him out of Stirling, out of his home?

Then he reconsidered. Wasn't that what Tristan wanted? Didn't he intend to strike out on his own?

Maybe Thomas had just given him the wee push that he needed.

"I see."

Thomas clenched Tristan's shoulder in his meaty grip. "I've loved ye like a son, MacKenzie. Ye know that."

Tristan choked down a lump in his throat. He nodded.

"But I think this is for the best, all things considered. With your talent, ye can find work anywhere. And if ye need any references, ye know where to find me."

Everything was happening so fast. The bread sat in his stomach like a lead weight. He'd been at Stirling since he was a turnbrochie. It was hard to think of leaving.

And yet he wouldn't be leaving alone. He'd have beautiful Mery Graham, soon to be Mery MacKenzie, by his side. They'd throw their fortunes together and embark on a new adventure, hand in hand.

Thomas clapped his hands and rubbed his palms together. "Now, if ye were just handfasted, won't ye be needin' a fine feast to celebrate?"

As it turned out, at the end of the day, Thomas loaded him up with dishes to take back to the Mar house—enough to feed an army. He bid the kitchen staff a sad farewell and gave Easson's hair a fond tousle. Then he left for the spectacle shop, laden like a packhorse.

When Mery greeted him at the door, her bright smile made him instantly forget any regrets he harbored about leaving Stirling. How rewarding it would be to come home to her shining face every day, no matter where they lived.

Her sparkling eyes roved over his packages.

"What's all this?" she crooned.

"The handfastin' feast."

"Did ye make it?"

"Some of it."

"It smells wonderful."

She helped him pack the food upstairs. They invited the Mar family to join them. Over the next hour they stuffed themselves on mutton chuets, duck with cloves, boiled cabbage, roast capons, leek pottage, coneys with mustard sauce, baked wardens, and cream custard. The master cook had even thrown in a bottle of fine Madeira for them to share.

Alisoune and Lachlan said it was the best meal they'd ever had. Even the children were swallowing every last bite of their supper. Tristan felt like he was grinning from ear to ear.

The kindly couple had promised them the upstairs all to themselves tonight. Tristan could hardly wait.

The first time he'd coupled with Mery had been in haste on a kitchen table. The second had been against a garden wall. The third had been on a cold, hard bench.

He wanted to make love to her at his leisure in a real bed. She deserved that much. Besides, he had a few surprises he'd saved for just the two of them.

Perched on the edge of the bed, Mery felt like a spoiled kitten with a bowl full of cream. There were so many delicious possibilities ahead of her. She hardly knew where to begin.

She tucked her lip under her teeth as she eyed the glazed pescod puffs and jewel-bright jellies, the peppery gingerbread squares and sweet sugared almonds, the pink quince marmalade and velvety golden custard, the fluffy white meringues and glistening cherry tarts.

"Well?" Tristan asked, kneeling before her with the tray.

As she studied the tasty array of delicacies, she knew the most tempting sweet of all wasn't on the dish.

Without a word, she took the tray from him and set it on the table beside the bed. Then she caught his face between her hands and lowered her gaze to his mouth.

"This," she said. "This is the sweet I want."

She bent forward and placed a soft kiss on his lips. She felt him smile.

He returned her affections, tangling his fingers in her hair to tip her head and deepen the kiss.

She sighed into his mouth, casting aside her spectacles and closing her eyes against the firelight. He tasted like joy and desire and worship combined.

As he continued to kiss her, he withdrew his hands from her hair. He caught the shell of her ears between his thumb and fingers, circling the outer rims and pulling gently at the lobes. She felt her whole body shiver with passion.

He moved his hands lower, grazing her neck with the back of his knuckles. Then his fingers drifted across her shoulders to linger at the edges of her gown.

She dared to slip her tongue out, lapping tentatively at the rim of his lips. He caught her tongue with his own, swirling around it, then pushing gently inside her mouth.

She chuckled deep in her throat and opened her mouth to engage him. She delved her hands into his lush hair, coiling the locks around her fingers.

Her breath caught as he teased the neck of her gown lower, inch by fraction of an inch. She grew hot as his callused fingertips created sensuous friction everywhere they brushed the sensitive skin of her bosom.

She broke from the kiss then, arching her neck to encourage his trespass.

But he wouldn't be commanded. His fingers retreated to the tops of her shoulders, resting benignly atop her stomacher.

Her brow creased. She wanted him. Didn't he know that?

She dragged her hands across his stubbled jaw and down to his throat. With her thumb, she could feel his pulse, strong and steady. She slid her fingers under his doublet and shirt to trace the rigid edges of his collar bone.

Perhaps if she kissed him again...

She leaned forward, pressing her lips to his with a hum of pleasure.

He replied by clenching his hands around her shoulders.

She locked her arms around his neck, drawing him close.

He moved his hands slowly down her sides, as if he counted each rib. Only when he reached the last did he bring his hands together at her waist.

But she longed to have him touch her breasts. Was that not obvious? She was offering him her bosom. Yet every time she thrust toward him, he retreated.

Maybe if she made advances on him...

She began unfastening his doublet, kissing each spot as she revealed more and more of his glorious chest. When it was undone, she shoved it off of his shoulders. But it stopped at his elbows, trapping his arms.

She gave him a sultry smile. Maybe it was better this way. Now she could have her way with him.

She held his arms where they were. Using her teeth, she

dragged his linen shirt off of one shoulder, then bathed his burning flesh with her tongue. She felt his arms tense, though she wasn't sure whether her light caress tickled or pleased him.

She repeated the process with his other shoulder, laving him thoroughly. When she dipped her tongue into the crease between his chest and his arm, he shivered.

His chest rose and fell more rapidly now. The idea that she was exciting him excited her in turn.

She lunged forward like a wolf on the hunt to savage his throat. The skin of his neck was hot, soft, vulnerable. She gnawed gently at the place where his heart pounded. He grimaced, but it was a grimace of lust. He tipped his head farther, granting her access.

When she nipped the lobe of his ear, he growled as if she were an errant pup. He'd had enough.

With a shrug of his shoulders, he loosened her grip and tore the doublet from his arms. Then, gazing at her with a wicked smirk, he repaid her in kind.

He swiftly unlaced her stomacher and spread it wide until it locked her arms in place. His teeth rasped across her skin as he drew the linen off of her shoulder. He sampled every inch of her exposed flesh with his tongue.

Then he moved to the other side. She turned her head, biting her lip as he bathed her, then blew a light breath across her shoulder.

She gasped in delicious shock when he attacked her throat. She squirmed as his tongue traced a path up the side of her neck toward her ear. The anticipation was sweet torment. A warm vibration surged in her veins, circling her head. When he caught her lobe tenderly between his teeth, the current snaked through her whole body, making sparks.

But he wasn't done. She squeezed her eyes tightly, struggling halfheartedly to free her arms, as he moved to the other side.

Her heart throbbed. Her nerves sang. This time when his tongue teased a wet trail toward her ear, she sobbed at the burning need that flooded her veins. And when he ensnared her lobe with soft lips, she felt the sparks of desire flare to life.

She burned for him. Every nerve roused at his touch. Yet he still hadn't ventured past the lowered neckline of her underdress.

How could he not know what she desired?

Once he released her arms, she whipped out of the sleeves of her stomacher. Now there was only linen between them.

Leading the way, she split the opening of his shirt and nuzzled the flesh there, moving toward the taut muscle of his male breast and the tender nipple that crowned it. She sucked lovingly while his hands rose to cup her head in encouragement.

Satisfied, she slid back the other side of his shirt and fed on its twin. She licked him to a hard point as he grunted softly against her hair.

Finally, supporting her head in one palm, he used the other on her shoulder to tip her backwards onto the bed.

Now they were getting somewhere.

Making love to one's bride was like dining on a fine meal, Tristan decided. She might be hungry, even ravenous. But gobbling down everything at once was not the best way to enjoy it.

What they'd done before had been satisfying enough, the way that gulping down a crust of bread filled an empty belly.

But Mery was his wife now. She was the woman he loved. She deserved to have the best experience he could provide.

A well-arranged supper started with wee nibbles and light fare. It should tempt without satisfying, tease without spoiling, and hint at the dishes to come.

And so he'd given Mery a sample—a soft kiss here, a subtle caress there—just enough to whet her appetite.

He could see she wanted more. Hell, he wanted more. But it was unwise to rush into gorging on the first course when there was so much more to come.

It wouldn't be easy for him. He was already as hot and iron-hard as a turnbrochie's spit.

His lips twitched as he gazed down at the bonnie lass lolling on the bed. She couldn't have thrust her bosom any higher. It was painfully obvious she yearned to have him touch her there.

He wasn't going to. Not yet. That was for the second course. There were plenty of other dishes to sample first.

Reaching under her arms, he lifted her up a few inches and dragged her completely onto the bed. Then he sat beside her.

He picked up her hand and held it between his two. With a deceptively innocent smile, he kissed the tip of each finger.

She sighed and smiled back.

He repeated the process, but this time he took the end of each of her fingers between his lips, tasting the flesh by briefly swirling his tongue over each sensitive tip.

Her eyes dipped.

He gave her a lascivious grin. Then he eyed the tray of sweets. "A meringue or a jelly?" he murmured, trying to decide. "A jelly, I think."

He picked one of the sticky red sweets from the tray and opened her hand, placing it in her palm.

Next, he spread her fingers. Then he lowered his head to slowly lap up the jelly, covering her palm with his tongue and licking at the webbing between her fingers. He slipped her fingers, one by one, fully into his mouth, sucking the jelly from each digit.

She made a soft whimper.

"Mmm," he replied, gazing against at the tray. "Now what?" He chose a meringue, placing the wee white cloud on the inside bend of her elbow. "Perfect."

Again, he bent his head, opening his mouth around the meringue. He let it dissolve on his tongue as he swept it over the delicate skin of her inner arm.

She gulped.

When it was almost gone, he let her share the last of it, moving up to kiss her on the lips, letting the sugar mingle in their mouths.

"What next?" he whispered against her cheek.

She was too enraptured to answer.

"A pescod," he decided. He lifted one of the shiny pillows of dough from the tray. "Here," he said, using a finger on her chin to turn her head aside. He placed the pescod on her neck, just below her ear.

She crinkled her eyes shut expectantly, which made him

chuckle. But it didn't stop him from diving onto the pescod, nibbling at the sweet puff and her neck all at once.

She was panting now. Her eyes were full of smoke and hunger. Soon he would feed the lusting beast inside her...if he could hold out long enough.

# CHAPTER 29

ery felt like every nerve was on fire. How had he done it? How did he know precisely where to place his warm lips, where to touch her, where to lick her, to ignite her body in such a way?

She thought she'd wanted him before. But that gentle yearning was nothing to what she felt now. Now she wanted to cover herself with sweets so that he'd devour her.

As if he could read her thoughts, he gave her a sly smile. She held her breath as he used his thumbs to peel away the linen of her underdress, carefully unwrapping her like a precious package.

His eyes were glazed with desire as he lowered them to her bared breasts. Her bosom heaved with longing, and she begged him with her gaze to touch her.

He whispered, "Next, the custard."

He plucked the bowl from the tray, setting it beside her on the bed. Then he dipped his finger into the smooth golden cream and brought it to her lips. She sucked the sweet substance from his finger, marveling at the silken texture.

He dipped his finger again, and this time he drizzled the thick cream onto her breast. She shivered as he bent his head for a thorough taste. A moan was wrung from her as he drew her nipple into his mouth, warming her flesh and quickening her loins.

Her hands clenched the coverlet as he repeated the ritual for her other breast, bringing her to a fine point of desire.

But still she wasn't satisfied. Now the place between her legs ached with an even fiercer need. When she tried to arch against him, she brushed the clear evidence of his lust. He was rock-hard and ready. And that brief contact sent a shudder through him—a shudder that made her feel strangely powerful.

Suddenly inspired, she wrapped her legs around his thighs and pushed at his shoulders until he rolled sideways, falling onto his back on the bed. Now she was the aggressor. Bare to the waist and straddling him, she felt like a goddess riding atop some great mythical beast.

He groaned with ecstasy as she pressed against him. She might be inexperienced. But it was blatantly obvious what pleased him.

With mischief on her mind, she pulled his shirt up to expose his chest, stomach, and the bulge in his breeches. Mimicking him, she dipped her finger into the custard and dripped it over his nipple. Then, with a coy smile, she swept her hair aside and lowered her head, letting him watch through slit lids as she enjoyed every last drop.

When she was finished with one, she dined on the other. Though he tried to remain stoic, she felt his rising lust as it manifested beneath her.

Then she spied the cherry tart.

With a wicked grin, she picked up the pastry and plopped it upside down on his stomach.

He jerked in surprise. "What the devil?"

"Oh, dear," she breathed. "I've made a mess."

Sticky syrup pooled on his stomach and threatened to drip down his sides.

"Ye're an imp," he said, "ye know that?"

"Oh, aye," she admitted, arching a brow. "So I've heard." For a moment, she only looked down at the glistening ruby-colored liquid adorning the sculpted contours of his stomach. His arms were bent. His hands were clenched. But he was trapped on his back, at her mercy.

"Ye'd best lie very still," she warned. "We don't want to stain the sheets."

"Whate'er ye intend, lass," he growled, "ye'd better hurry."

What she intended was lapping up every bit of the excess. She slurped cherries from his quivering belly, licking her lips as the fruit burst inside her mouth.

"Mmm. Ye've outdone yourself with this cherry tart, MacKenzie," she teased. "'Tis most delectable." She finished off the flaky pastry, sucking the crumbs from her fingers, and licked his flesh clean. Then she boldly brushed her tongue over his hip bone and was rewarded with a quiet groan. Sheer daring made her cluck her tongue. "Faith, I fear some may have escaped beneath your trews."

Breathless, he rose on his elbows and watched her through half-closed eyes.

She loosened the laces of his trews and pushed them down the tiniest bit, just enough to lick a few stray streaks of juice from his abdomen. And then she ventured a wee bit farther, edging the tip of her tongue toward the place where his hair grew thicker.

Finally, he could stand no more. With a lusty groan, he seized her wrists and rolled her over onto her back, pinning her hands to the bed.

But she wasn't afraid. Indeed, it was a heady feeling, knowing she'd driven him half mad with longing. She giggled, wondering what he'd do next.

"I think, lass, ye need a lesson in cookin'."

She raised her brows in surprise. "Do I?"

"Aye." Skewering her with a smoldering gaze, he joined her wrists above her head with one hand. "If ye insist on usin' such a hot flame, ye'll burn dinner."

"Will I?" She tucked her lip under her teeth, aroused by the lusty cast of his eyes.

With his free hand, he drew her skirts up, inch by painstaking inch. It seemed to take forever as she felt every thread cross her thigh.

"Ye have to have patience," he murmured. "A low flame. A slow simmer."

She held her breath as his fingers finally gathered the last bit of fabric and settled with a feather-light touch on the curls between her legs.

One corner of his lip curved up as he found her. "A watchful eye so ye know exactly when to stir the pot."

With that, he slipped his fingers tenderly between the petals of her womanhood.

She gasped and twisted in his grip. His sweet caress was the most curious paradox. He quenched her thirst. Yet he left her desiring more. She sought to evade his touch. Yet she craved it, enough to arch her hips toward him.

When she caught her breath, she muttered, "Now who's the wicked lad?"

He grinned, but there was vulnerability in his eyes that was intriguing and compelling. He was made as helpless by desire as she was.

"Ach, lass, ye're so delicious. I can hardly resist ye."

She lifted her head. "Well, for shite's sake, who's askin' ye to?"

He paused for only an instant. Then he shoved down the waist of his breeches and freed himself. He eased forward, sinking into her as smoothly as butter spread on bread.

Once he released her wrists, she twined her arms around his shoulders and burrowed her face against his neck. This time, when he began the ritual of lovemaking, it felt like the quiet beginning of a madrigal. Each slow, measured thrust invited the next. There was no chaos, no desperation, just a gradual and steady increase in intensity.

Together they sang, matching line for line. He added an embellishment here with a brush of his hand through her hair. She supplied a flourish there with a row of kisses across his throat. Though they sang the same melody, each brought their own voice to the music.

Every verse built upon the last. Like lines of counterpoint, the two of them wove together, separated, and met again. And each time they rejoined, the passion was stronger and the music more beautiful.

She thought it was truly the most exquisite song ever crafted, made all the more perfect by the fact that she shared it with the man who'd wed her.

Overcome by love and lust, she held tighter to him, sobbing against his throat as he transported her higher and higher toward the heavens. Deeper he plunged, filling her completely, his gasps rasping past her ear.

With a final cry of ecstasy, she vaulted into divine realms of sensation. He followed closely with a quiet roar of victory. And then they sighed together in perfect harmony, ending the music of their love with a hushed amen.

Tristan collapsed onto the bed beside his wife—his *wife*, he realized with amazement. How he'd managed to snag her, he didn't know. After all, the first time they'd met, he'd insulted her.

He smiled at the memory. Had it truly been less than a week ago? He realized he'd never really had the chance to offer her an apology for his crass comment.

"Mery," he whispered as they lay staring up at the ceiling, gasping in recovery.

"Aye?"

"I've been meanin' to tell ye somethin'."

"Don't say it," she guessed. "Ye're actually a satyr in man's clothin'."

He laughed. "Nae. I've been meanin' to say that on the morn we met, ye weren't really scarin' the fish."

She snorted. "I'm probably scarin' them tonight, though."

He chuckled. "True enough."

"Do ye think we woke the Mar children?"

"Nae," he said. "They're probably listenin' at the door."

She snickered.

He thought about how happy the Mar family was. Could he and Mery ever find that kind of contentment? Would Mery ever wish to settle down? Or would she tire of him and let wanderlust lure her away?

She threaded her fingers through his. "So how many children do ye think we'll have?" she asked.

"Children? We've been handfasted half a day, and ye're already talkin' about children?"

"Well, at the rate we're goin', if we do this two, three times a day..."

"Or five."

"Or five," she agreed with a grin. "We're goin' to have bairns sooner or later. So how many do ye think?"

"Well, let's see. If I'm to have my own staff, I'll need a turnbrochie, a couple o' lads to do the choppin', a half dozen cooks, at least one baker, and a confectioner for ye. I'd say an even dozen."

"Well, that's fine for the lads, but what about the lasses?"

"Ye can have some lasses, if ye like."

"I would. I'll need at least two altos and two sopranos. Can four o' your kitchen lads sing?"

"Ach, sure, as long as they've finished their kitchen chores."

She laughed and poked him in the ribs.

Then they grew serious.

"What *are* our plans?" she asked, turning on her side toward him.

He'd hoped to delay that conversation. But they couldn't stay at the Mar house forever. And he'd already said his farewells at the castle.

He sighed. "How would ye feel about leavin' Stirlin'?"

"Really?" She rose up on an elbow. To his surprise, she actually seemed relieved. "But this is your home. I know ye grew up here. And ye have a position at the castle."

He didn't want to tell her the truth—that Thomas Chalmers had practically banished him from the kitchens. Nor did he want her to know the real reason why—that the master cook thought he'd killed the tambor player. So he told her the other reason.

"To be honest, I'm weary o' servin' royals and bein' at the queen's beck and call. I have no kin left here. I'd like to light out on my own and see what comes of it."

He expected her to be disappointed. But she wasn't. In fact, her eyes lit up.

"So ye're up for a grand adventure?" she asked.

"Aye, I suppose so."

"Then we'll go on it together," she decided.

That pleased him. "Seize the day."

"Aye, seize the day. Do ye know where ye want to go?"

Ever since Thomas had suggested he go "far away," he'd been giving it some thought. "There's a tavern I know of at the Borders. 'Tis run by a lady who was once a spy for Queen Mary."

"A lady spy?" Mery's brows shot up. "Ye know a lady spy?"

"I don't really know her. But years ago, I cooked for her weddin' feast in Musselburgh, at the queen's request. 'Twas the first time I'd e'er made a banquet on my own."

"Do ye think she might let ye cook at her tavern?"

"I don't know," he admitted. "'Twas a long while ago. They liked my cookin'. But I can't be sure they're still there."

"I like the Borders," Mery mused. "What's the name o' the tavern?"

"The Rose and Thorn."

She sat up abruptly. "Not the MacAdams' place? Next to the links? By the sea?"

"Ye know it?"

"O' course I know it!" She beamed. "Drew MacAdam is a champion golfer, aye? I've sung at his tournaments a half dozen times."

"Ye have?"

"Aye, though I didn't know Josselin was a spy." She gave him a quizzical look. "I thought she was a tavern wench."

"That's no doubt what made her a good spy."

Mery's eyes sparkled as she clapped her hands with glee. "Oh, Tristan, I just know this is all goin' to work out. I can feel it in my heart. And my Ma always said ye can never go wrong if ye follow your heart."

He grinned. Tristan's heart was telling him to follow his adorable wife wherever she went. He sensed, whether they wound up in Edinburgh or Inveraray, Mery Graham would always feel like home to him.

# CHAPTER 30

**DECEMBER 21, 1567**
**THE ROSE AND THORN**

Mery peered out the window of their bedchamber at the blanket of fog rolling across the seashore. Today was the day.

She felt like a sow. When she and Tristan had been handfasted a year and a day ago, it had never occurred to her that she might be heavy with child when it came time for their wedding.

It was to be an intimate affair. Though church weddings had been required in some places since the Council of Trent, most Scots didn't abide by the new law, particularly this far away from anyone interested in enforcing it. Considering Mery's condition, she had little desire to waddle down the aisle of a church and no interest in kneeling repeatedly before an altar.

Instead, she chose a nearby village friar to perform the ceremony at the inn. Tristan planned to cook up a wedding feast at The Rose and Thorn for some of their friends. And Mery planned to squeeze into whatever gown would still encompass her enormous girth.

"Promise me somethin'," she said, turning to Tristan as she made a tiny bow in what was left of the laces of her burgundy-colored stomacher.

"What's that?"

How Tristan managed to gaze fondly down at her when she was the size of a small horse, she didn't know. But she loved him for it.

"Promise me ye won't mistake me for a pig and serve me up for supper."

He gave her nose a chiding tap. "Ye're a beautiful bride, Mery MacKenzie."

She smiled uncertainly. She hadn't felt beautiful for weeks now.

"Besides," he added, "we're havin' venison for supper."

"Rane shot a deer?"

"Aye, yesterday."

Deer were scarce in winter. But Rane MacFarland was an expert huntsman. He'd worked for the MacAdams, supplying game for The Rose and Thorn, for the past four years. He was a good man—a tall, fair-haired archer with Viking blood. He'd actually known Josselin MacAdam since she was a wee lass in Selkirk.

Tristan cupped Mery's face and placed a soft kiss on her lips. "I have a surprise for ye."

"A surprise?"

Before he could tell her what it was, a knock came on the door.

"Are ye dressed?" There was Jossy now.

"Come in," Mery called.

Jossy popped in her honey-blonde head. "I've come to steal your husband."

Mery clucked her tongue. "Already? We're not even properly wed yet."

Jossy gave her a wink. "The guests are already caterwaulin' for their breakfast, Tris. I'm afraid it makes no difference if 'tis your weddin' day."

"I'll be right down," Tristan told her, pulling on his boots.

Since they'd come last year, the MacAdams' tavern had grown into an inn, complete with lodging and meals. Even with a small complement of cooks to help him, Tristan kept busy in the kitchens.

Mery had found a place for herself as well. During the days, she kept watch over the MacAdams' three children while Jossy served up ale. At night, she performed in the tavern.

Of course, Drew's golf links and Jossy's signature beer had drawn guests to The Rose and Thorn. But now, with Tristan's culinary skills and Mery's singing added to the mix, the inn had become a popular destination. Because of its situation along the Borders, friendly folk—both Scottish and English—dropped in for a pint, a bite of pottage, or a round of golf, which was outlawed in England.

Mery was thankful for their friendship. Sadly, despite the message of peace and unity the baptism of Prince James had promised last December, politics between the two countries had grown more thorny than ever.

The queen had been wed in the spring to Lord Bothwell, which shocked everyone. After all, according to rumor, the lord had helped to murder Mary's previous husband, Lord Darnley, and had forced her into his bed. There were even claims that the queen's marriage to a Protestant lord wasn't legitimate under Catholic law.

By summer, tragedy struck. The unhappy nobles of Scotland imprisoned the pregnant Mary at Loch Leven Castle on charges of adultery and murder. She lost the twins she was carrying, and she was forced to abdicate the throne to her one-year-old son.

It seemed she and Tristan had left the castle just in time. Here along the Borders, simple folk didn't pay much heed to the politics of the far-off courts of Stirling or London.

"Ye look like ye're a hundred miles away," Tristan commented.

"Oh, aye, just thinkin' about Stirlin'."

"So much has changed," he said, shaking his head. "'Tis probably best I left when I did." He kissed her brow. "But I'm happy I took ye with me."

There was another knock on the door. "Mery?"

This time it was Florie MacFarland, Rane's wife.

"Come in," Tristan and Mery said together.

Florie was a stunning woman. Though she was old enough to have threads of white in her dark hair, her brown eyes sparkled like the jewels she crafted.

"I have somethin' for ye," she said to Mery, presenting her with a wee box tied with a blue ribbon.

"But ye already made us weddin' rings," Mery argued. The braided silver bands were in a box beside the bed. They planned to exchange them during the ceremony.

"'Tis only a wee trinket," Florie said.

With eager fingers, Mery opened the box. It was anything but a wee trinket. Inside was a breathtaking diamond-shaped ruby pendant. The jewel winked at her from a silver setting formed into the stem of a musical note.

Mery gasped. "'Tis a *fusa!*"

Tristan studied it. "'Tis a ladle."

She elbowed him. "Nae, 'tis a *fusa*, silly. 'Tis a note o' music. Ah, Florie, 'tis perfect."

"The ruby is for love," Florie said with a smile, helping clasp it around her neck. "I hope your marriage makes ye two as happy as we are."

She excused herself then, saying she had to make sure her twelve-year-old twins weren't annoying the guests.

"'Tis amazin' those two are happy at all," Tristan remarked after she'd left, "considerin' he shot her when they first met." Her archer husband had mistaken her for a deer and fired an arrow into her thigh.

She shrugged. "I suppose it could have been worse. He could have told her she was scarin' the fish."

He shook his head. She was never going to let him forget his insult.

"Well, I'd better go below before the starvin' guests start to eat one another."

"I'll be down in a wee bit," she promised.

It was only after he left that she realized he hadn't told her what the surprise was.



Tristan was glad to be running the kitchens on his wedding day. He wouldn't know what to do with himself if he didn't have something simmering on the fire. He realized cooking was as much a part of his everyday life as singing was to Mery's.

His four trusty cooks made the work easy. They were

efficient and enthusiastic, and they enjoyed trying out his new ideas. He'd promised them a trip to Stirling later this year so they could see what the royal kitchens were like. He wanted to visit his old friends, especially Thomas Chalmers, who must be cooking now for the new king.

Breakfast for the guests this morn was three different kinds of bread served with butter, sage, and honey, along with Jossy's small ale. But the venison for dinner was already roasting. There was pottage bubbling on the hearth. And the cooks would be working all morn, creating the tempting assortment of sweets he'd planned for Mery.

Of course, since The Rose and Thorn was a public inn, their wedding feast would have to include a number of stray guests who happened to be staying there. But Tristan didn't mind. He didn't suppose Mery did either. Both of them enjoyed sharing their talents with strangers. Besides, the good reports from travelers about the food and the entertainment kept the inn thriving.

He was halfway through stirring the redcurrant sauce for the venison when he realized he'd never told Mery about her surprise. He supposed she'd find out soon enough.

"MacKenzie," Drew MacAdam said by way of a greeting as he entered the kitchens. His hair was damp and his face ruddy from the cold outdoors.

"MacAdam," Tristan replied. "What brings ye to the kitchens this morn?"

"Have you got a crust o' somethin' for me? I just finished a round, and I'm famished."

Tristan grinned, handing him a thick slice of oaten bread. No doubt Drew MacAdam would golf every day, even in a thunderstorm with the water up to his knees.

"Ye *will* take a moment to come to my weddin'?"

He winked. "Wouldn't miss it." He took the bread with a nod of thanks and strode off.

The friar arrived early, no doubt because Tristan had promised him a hearty breakfast. Tristan seated him with the MacAdam and MacFarland children.

One by one, the guests came down to break their fast. Some of them left, eager to be on the road. Others took a look at the gloomy day and decided to linger. Finally, his bride made her way down the stairs.

"What would ye like for breakfast, beloved?" he called to her. "Pickled eels? Smoked oysters?"

Mery's tastes had gone to extremes since she'd been pregnant. It was challenging, trying to come up with dishes she felt like eating.

She wrinkled her nose. "Could ye make me eggs?"

"For my darlin' bride, aye," he said, helping her to a seat. "'Twill be just a moment."

Before he could return to the kitchens, the door of the inn opened, letting in the cool mist and something else.

"Ah! Here's your surprise, Mery," Tristan said.

Mery's eyed widened in wonder when she saw the two travelers with bags. "Alisoune? Lachlan?"

"And me!" announced Copernica, popping out from behind them.

Alisoune's spectacles immediately fogged up, and she took them off, polishing them with her sleeve. "Mery, ye're lookin'..." She put her spectacles back on and gave a start. "Faith! Ye're lookin' ready to propagate!"

"Congratulations," Lachlan said.

Mery thanked him, resting her hands on her enlarged abdomen. "But what are ye doin' here?"

"We came for your nuptials, o' course," Alisoune said.

"All the way from Stirlin'?"

"We couldn't miss your weddin'," Lachlan said. "After all, we were part of the handfastin'."

"What a wonderful surprise," Mery said as they closed the door behind them, set down their bags, and shrugged off their cloaks.

Tristan took a few moments to introduce everyone.

Jossy took an immediate interest in Lachlan's mechanical leg. She asked him about his sword technique and whether he'd had to adjust his style to accommodate the metal appendage.

Drew was fascinated by Alisoune's spectacles. He wondered if there was a lens that could make the distant holes on the links easier to see.

Rane came in the door then, and wee Copernica nearly jumped out of her skin as the towering giant loomed above her like a Viking invader, a brace of coneys slung over his broad shoulder.

He nodded to Tristan, who took the coneys off his hands.

Then Rane's wife, Florie, swooped in in her disarming fashion, patting Rane's chest as if to prove to the wee lass that the Viking was all muscle, but no fright.

Once Florie spotted the unique pendant around Alisoune's neck, she took her by the elbow into the light to get a better look. To her amazement, it turned out Florie had crafted the rainbow crystal piece when she was an apprentice in her father's goldsmith shop in Selkirk. Alisoune and Lachlan remembered her, and though Florie hadn't recalled Lachlan's mechanical leg, she remembered their big shaggy deerhound.

Soon, Lachlan and Jossy were discussing battlefield strategy. Alisoune and Drew talked about the mathematical art of golf. Copernica entertained the other children with a lecture about the characteristics of fire. Rane, ever generous, consulted the friar to see if there were any villagers in need of food. And Tristan cooked up Mery's plate of eggs, sprinkled with dill and parsley and served with a cup of weak ale.

Mery smiled. It looked like everyone was getting along. This was exactly how she wanted to spend her wedding— surrounded by close friends.

Meanwhile, travelers came and went. Some huddled by the fire. Some leaned against the wall for a small beer and a quick nap. It never rained, but the fog drifted back and forth, coming in like a curious cat to sniff at the inn, then retreating to the shoreline.

Finally, there was a lull in the morn's commotion, and the friar asked if everyone was ready to begin.

Florie, having a marvelous eye for design, had planned most of the details. She'd already draped garlands of holly from the rafters and had the twins place extra candles about the tavern. Now she directed Rane and Drew in moving the tables to make room for the ceremony. She gave the children blossoms of dried heather to scatter among the rushes.

Jossy served a last round of beer to the travelers, warning them they'd have to wait until after the wedding for more. Tristan promised everyone a plate for the feast to come, which helped alleviate any disappointment they might have had.

Then all the friends gathered round while Mery took her place on Tristan's left. The friar took a breath to begin.

"Shite," whispered Tristan, patting his doublet. "Just a moment."

Snickers traveled through the crowd as Tristan took the stairs two at a time to fetch the rings from their bedchamber.

When he returned, the ceremony began.

Mery and Tristan repeated the vows they'd made a year and a day ago, this time binding their words with the exchange of their woven silver rings.

Mery's gift to Tristan was her own rendition of *A ce matin,* a slightly bawdy French song detailing the lovely dishes on which she'd like to dine to satisfy *all* of her earthly appetites.

Tristan said his gift to Mery would come after the meal, which sparked speculative groans from the rest of the couples.

Then Florie threw a white tablecloth across three trestle tables set end to end and decorated them with candles and holly. The kitchen staff brought out the most impressive feast ever seen at The Rose and Thorn. The wedding guests enjoyed a savory splurge of venison with redcurrants, stewed hens with lemons, pigeon pie, trout in cider, and roast coney—food fit for a queen.

The cooks even brought out thick pottage and barley bread for the children and guests for whom the food was too rich.

After the last course, Tristan presented his gift to Mery—a gigantic tray of every kind of confection imaginable.

She gasped, then laughed. How well her husband knew her.

On the tray were cinnamon-sprinkled pescod puffs,

gingerbread topped with green and scarlet marchpane, shiny gooseberry tarts, burgundy wine jellies, spiced damson pudding, chuets of minced veal and sultanas, quince and orange compote, gingered applemoise, sugared almonds, feather-light meringues, preserved figs, and honeyed dates.

In truth, Mery's belly was so full of food and bairn that she couldn't eat many of the treats. But she enjoyed the expressions on the faces of those around her, particularly the children, as they sampled the heavenly sweets.

Her gaze softened as she looked at the man who had made them. He would forever be the sweetest thing in her life.

# CHAPTER 31

More than the generous praise and raves from the guests, Tristan was moved by his bride's loving glance. For her, he would slave all day over a hellish fire. For her, he would work long hours in smoke and sweat. For her...

The door of the inn swung open, letting in a chill wave of air and a traveler bundled against the cold. Ordinarily, Tristan paid no mind to the strangers who came and went at The Rose and Thorn. They were usually gone in a day or two and not worth remembering.

But even in the midst of the hubbub, this one caught his eye.

There was nothing remarkable about him. He had a slight hunch to his back, and his cloak was pulled around his brown-bearded face. But something drew Tristan's attention to the man.

"Isn't that true, Tristan?" Mery was saying.

The man's head lifted at the sound of Tristan's name—only an inch—yet that gesture was troubling.

"What's that, my love?" he asked, still eyeing the

traveler as he made his way to the tavern counter.

"Didn't ye say my voice scared the fish?"

"I did," he admitted sheepishly to his friends, who hooted at him in disapproval.

His gaze wandered back to the stranger, who was now leaning on the counter. Jossy got up from where she was sitting to wait on him.

Something bothered him about that man. He couldn't put his finger on it. And the fact that Jossy had gone to talk to him troubled him more. He'd have to ask her what he'd said.

When she returned to the table, he made an excuse to circle the long table, talking to each of his friends in turn.

When he got to Jossy, he murmured, "What did that bearded man want?"

She shrugged. "A beer."

"Is that all?"

"Aye."

"Did ye notice anythin'...odd...about him?"

"Odd?" She shook her head. "He's French. Is that odd?"

Tristan frowned. He didn't have many French acquaintances. He had French kin on his mother's side. But he didn't know any of them. Maybe his worry was for nothing.

He spoke to a few others, occasionally glancing at the man while he sipped his beer. Then he returned to his seat while the loud conversations around the table continued.

"But he once chased after the nobles in Queen Mary's court with a whip," Mery was saying. "Didn't ye, Tristan?"

He opened his mouth to reply, then froze.

All at once, it hit him.

He knew who the stranger was.

The man stiffened.

Was that Tristan MacKenzie, the bloody cook from Stirling Castle? What were the odds?

Ever since he'd bungled the assassination of Queen Mary's brat, he'd been on the run. Only now he was *everyone's* enemy. Worse, the prince he could have strangled in his crib was now king.

After tangling with that damned cook and barely escaping Stirling with his life, he'd managed to evade capture by changing his identity every few days.

But when he'd finally arrived in England, he discovered it wasn't only the Scots who were after him. The Earl of Bedford had decided he was a mad man, uncontrollable and dangerous to the cause.

A "loose cannon," the earl had called him.

Now his only hope of redemption, his only chance to get back into the queen's good graces, was to do something of dramatic consequence, something that would give her a huge political advantage. Which was why he'd come to The Rose and Thorn.

He'd learned the proprietor of the inn, Josselin MacAdam, had once been a spy for Queen Mary. Her husband, Highlander Drew MacAdam, was actually Andrew Armstrong, an English turncoat. Most significant, the inn's location along the Scottish Borders made it an ideal spot to launch a network of spies to infiltrate England.

He suspected Jossy hadn't retired from service after all.

If so, and if he could expose The Rose and Thorn as a den of Scots spies—the taproot from which the limbs of espionage branched into England—the queen might forgive him for mucking up the Stirling matter. And if he yanked that tree out by its roots himself, the branches would wither, and he'd be given the credit he was due.

But with the Stirling cook in his way...

What the hell was *he* doing here anyway?

He was fairly sure MacKenzie hadn't recognized him. After all, he was very good at disguises. The Stirling inhabitants had only seen him as an excitable, mincing fop. They'd never expect such a thorough transformation. He'd grown out his beard, spoke in gruff French, affected a limp.

Still, he didn't dare risk discovery. He sank deeper into the shadows, holding his mug of beer in front of his face.

Someone cried out, "Here's to the bride and groom!"

That explained the gathering. Someone was having a wedding feast. Or at least that was what it was supposed to look like. A wedding feast could easily conceal a convergence of spies and an exchange of information.

"To the bride and groom!" everyone echoed.

MacKenzie came to his feet, locking his arm around the woman beside him and kissing the top of her head.

The man stared into his beer. Had MacKenzie really just gotten married? Or was he only portraying a groom? And who was the bride?

He peered over the top of his beer and suddenly tasted the bitter hops at the back of his throat.

Nae. It couldn't be. Not *that* woman, he thought, scowling at another stroke of misfortune. It was the cook's lover, the minstrel who he claimed had drunk the poison intended for the prince. And she was so pregnant, she looked like an over-inflated bagpipe.

He couldn't believe she'd survived. Dwale was powerful poison. But then he'd only used a few drops, just enough to kill an infant. She must have caught it in time.

Still, what was he going to do about her?

More than even the royals in both countries, these two wanted him dead.

He thought quickly about his options.

He had no petard this time, which was a shame. Even if it meant his own demise, if he managed to blow up an entire network of foreign spies with one petard, Queen Elizabeth would probably memorialize him as a political martyr.

He could slip quietly away and report his findings. But he had no proof that this was anything but a festive wedding celebration at a simple inn. And if he was wrong, he would become the laughingstock of the English court.

He could steal off and forget what he'd seen. He'd be no worse off than he was now, but no better either. He'd still be on the run, dogged at every turn by those who wanted him wiped off the face of the earth.

He could sweep away his disguise and confront them, relying on his bravado to catch them off guard and perhaps trick them into admitting they were indeed spies. But if the guests were allies of the cook, they outnumbered him. He'd be inviting a massacre.

Or...he could use leverage.

He twisted the poison ring around his knuckle.

Tristan's heart grew cold.

The man in the corner had a heavy beard and a pronounced stoop. He was half-hidden behind a voluminous cloak, and he'd spoken to Jossy in French.

He doubted if Mery, Lachlan, or Alisoune would recognize him.

But the bastard's features were engraved on Tristan's brain. And the ring he was turning on his finger was a poison ring, probably the same one he'd used at Stirling.

Tristan had to do something. He didn't intend to let the villain escape this time.

He wouldn't make the mistake of making eye contact. The inn was packed with people. He didn't want to endanger anyone else.

Whatever he did, it would have to be stealthy.

While the guests continued making toasts, he kept his arm protectively around Mery and murmured against her hair. "Do as I say. Go upstairs. And don't open the door for—"

She pulled away from him, arching a brow in challenge. He'd apparently forgotten who she was...again.

"What's goin' on?" she demanded.

"There's no time. Just do as I say."

"And if I don't?"

"Please, Mery," he pleaded. "'Tisn't safe here. Think o' the bairn."

"Tell me what's goin' on."

It was pointless arguing with her. Mery was fearless and stubborn.

But she was also bright. Maybe if he told her, she'd agree that going upstairs was her best option.

He sighed. "The man in the corner—don't look at him—

is the one who poisoned ye." Her gaze half strayed toward the corner, but he snapped it back with a sharp, "Nae!"

"The tambor player?" she mumbled, her brows furrowed. "But ye said he was dead."

Tristan bit back a curse. He should have realized his half-truth would catch up with him one day. He hadn't really said the villain was dead. He'd just let everyone believe that.

"He's not dead," she guessed, leveling him with a stare that was equal parts disbelief, anger, hurt, and fear.

He'd have to explain later. For now, he had to keep her safe.

"Please go upstairs. This is my fault. I'm goin' to finish what I should have finished a year ago."

"Ye can't do it alone."

He glanced around the table at his allies—a master archer, a seasoned soldier, and a man who wielded a wicked golf club. "I'm not alone."

He could see she didn't want to go upstairs. Whether it was because she didn't want to miss anything, didn't want to watch her husband die, or wanted to kill the man herself, he didn't know.

But in the end, common sense won out. Now that she was responsible for the bairn inside her, he found she wasn't quite as reckless as she'd once been, for which he was grateful.

The others teased Mery as she made her way up the stairs, telling her she'd forgotten her husband. She played along with them, offering up some clever retort.

Tristan didn't hear what it was. He'd gone to the kitchens to fetch his biggest butcher's knife.

# CHAPTER 32

The instant the minstrel went up the stairs and the cook headed for the kitchen, the man knew he'd been found out.

Bloody hell. He couldn't risk discovery. It was one thing to be hunted, quite another to be caught. If he was caught, he'd be executed as a traitor, drawn and quartered, his head stuck on a spike. He touched his poison ring for reassurance. He'd never let them take him alive.

MacKenzie had unwittingly left him a source of leverage. This might be the stroke of luck he needed. The man's wife would be easy to corner upstairs.

Still, there wasn't much time.

Leaving his beer on the table, he casually rose and made his way toward the steps. The merrymakers, still reveling in their feast, paid him no mind. All except one small girl with sharp eyes, sitting with the other children.

"Mama!" she called out in discovery. "Look! 'Tis the man with the petard!"

Her final word hung in the air, bringing the room to

silence for one sliver of a moment. And then the world came crashing down with a roar.

"Petard!" someone shouted.

Everyone shot to their feet. Two travelers panicked and ran out the door.

"Where, Copernica?" the girl's mother demanded.

The little girl damned him with a point of her finger.

He might have shown them his empty hands then. He could have shrugged off the accusation as the wild imagination of a child.

But the child's father had taken her at her word. With death in his eyes, he charged forward on his mechanical leg.

Desperate, the man grabbed the closest hostage at hand, a small boy. He whisked the lad up in one arm and wrapped an arm around his throat.

The serving wench who'd brought him the beer earlier yelled out, "Fight, Robbie!"

The child thrashed and struggled against him, landing a painful but not incapacitating kick in his groin. But when the boy took a bite out of his forearm, he dropped him with a curse and limped off.

In the meantime, the boy's mother had somehow gotten hold of a sword.

Muttering, "I've got this," to the man with the metal leg, she shoved him out of the way and took his place, brandishing her blade with the fury of a hen defending her chick.

There was no choice but to back away.

Suddenly he felt a sharp, piercing pain in the back of his upper arm, then his shoulder, then his neck. He wheeled. A pretty, dark-haired woman was stabbing him with a jeweled brooch.

He pushed her, hard enough to knock her on her arse at the feet of a man who looked like a Viking warrior, an angry Viking warrior.

The Viking's nostrils flared as he picked up a bow from against the wall and fitted an arrow into it.

"Back away, Jossy," he said to the tavern wench with the sword. "He's mine."

What was the Viking thinking? He couldn't shoot a bow inside of the inn.

Nonetheless, he seemed intent on doing just that. So before he could become the victim of an arrow through the heart, he hurtled toward the exit.

Just before he reached the door, the bespectacled woman poured something across his path. His foot slipped in the oily substance, and he was suddenly slammed to the floor.

Not a moment too soon. An arrow whizzed over his head and landed with a solid thunk in the wood of the door.

He scrambled to his feet, slipping and sliding. The man with the mechanical leg moved to block the exit. There was nowhere to go but upstairs.

Dodging tankards and tarts that were now being flung at him, he stumbled through the throng. A splotch of preserves dripped down his cheek. A spoonful of cheesecake struck his chest. Applemoise landed in his hair.

But he'd almost made it to the stairs.

"Nae!" came a roar as MacKenzie entered the room. He raised a lethal-looking butcher's knife. His eyes shone with dark fire.

But there was nowhere else to go. He climbed the first step.

"Don't let him up the stairs!" MacKenzie bellowed.

Suddenly, his legs were knocked out from under him. He went down like a shot, his chin hitting the steps, hard. Then the world faded to black.

The last thing he heard was the faint, smug echo of a Highland golfer yelling out, "Fore!"

Mery could hear a commotion downstairs. Normally, curiosity would have compelled her to see what was going on, no matter what she'd promised Tristan.

But she was afraid to move.

There had been a strange popping sensation inside of her, and now a trickle of warm water was dribbling onto the floor.

Was it time for the bairn to be born? Or had something gone wrong? Was she going to lose her child?

She didn't know what to do.

If her friends were facing off against the spy, she didn't dare distract them. And in her vulnerable state, she realized she could easily become a victim, which would complicate matters further.

But she couldn't just stand here, waiting for something awful to happen.

There was a lull in the noise now. Maybe it was safe to come down.

She made her slow and careful way across the room and peered out the door.

The inn was a mess. Chairs were overturned. Crockery was broken. Food had been flung everywhere. But it looked like the battle was over.

The guests were all chattering at once, puffing out their

chests and gesturing with their weapons. Florie had gathered up the children and was trying to distract them from the grisly sight at the bottom of the stairs. Rane pulled an arrow from the door. Alisoune polished her spectacles. Jossy sheathed her sword.

The spy—at least, Mery *assumed* it was the spy, for he looked very different from what she remembered—was sprawled on the first four steps. He was covered with splatters of food that dripped onto the stairs. But beneath his beard, he was deathly pale, breathless, and unmoving.

Then she saw Tristan. He was sitting on a bench, trembling from the ordeal as he stared into the fire. He'd stuck his big butcher's knife into the table. But Mery didn't think that was what had killed the spy. There didn't seem to be any blood on the knife or on the stairs. As she watched him, he raked his hand back through his hair and blew out a long, shaky breath.

She stepped through the door and was about to call out to him, to reassure him she was safe, when a dull pain throbbed in her back, halting her in her tracks.

Was it the bairn? Was it on its way? Or was it in danger?

The pain lessened, and she took a few cautious steps forward. She looked down the stairs. How she'd get around the body at the bottom, she didn't know. But first she had to contend with the half dozen stairs at the top.

One by one, she made her way down the steps. On the fourth, the pain seized her again. She braced herself against the wall, waiting for it to pass.

When she drew even with the spy's body, she wrinkled her nose in distaste. She hoped someone would move his gruesome remains out of the way.

She took a breath, intending to call out to Tristan again.

Suddenly, a hand closed around her ankle. Screaming with fright, she tried to shake it loose. But she lost her footing on the stair. Her second foot slipped as well. She fell back, banging her elbow. The sharp edge of the stair struck her back with numbing force.

Like a spider awakened by a struggling fly in its web, the spy came to life all at once, clambering over her until he perched on the stairs above her.

By the time everyone rushed forward in concern, the spy already had an arm around her neck and a sharp dagger at her throat.

She froze as she felt the prick of the stiletto.

Jossy and Lachlan drew their swords again, though they were useless while she was held at knifepoint. Drew smacked his golf club against his palm, equally frustrated. Rane nocked an arrow to his bow, but she knew he couldn't get off a clean shot.

Tristan wrenched his butcher's knife from the table. His fist tightened on the haft as his mouth worked with rage.

"Let me go!" the spy spat at them.

He prodded Mery with the stiletto. She winced as he drew blood.

"Let me go," he repeated, "and I'll let her live."

Mery felt a wave of pain coming again. She didn't dare writhe with the contraction. He might pierce her with the blade.

"Back away!" he shouted.

Everyone did as he said, though none of them looked happy about it.

Then, inch by awkward inch, they moved down the stairs together. He still held her in a viselike grip. One slip of her foot, and she'd be impaled on the slender blade.

The pain was about to start. She moaned against its coming.

She squeezed her eyes tightly as the ache started low in her back, working its way over her abdomen, grinding the way a heavy stone ground wheat.

By the time it subsided, sweat peppered her brow, and they'd reached the floor.

She glanced at Tristan, whose gaze was fixed with raw hate upon the spy.

This was her fault. She should have done as he'd asked. She should have stayed in their bedchamber. He was right. She was too stubborn for her own good. And now that stubbornness could very well get her killed...her and their unborn child.

# CHAPTER 33

Tristan's stare was so filled with cold fury that it should have pierced the spy's wicked heart by now.

But perhaps the villain didn't have a heart. How could he? He'd been willing to poison an innocent infant. He'd threatened to throttle a child. And now he was holding a pregnant woman at knifepoint.

To make matters worse, Tristan had seen the anguish crossing Mery's features a moment ago. Unless he was mistaken, she was in the first stages of labor.

He had to get her out of the bastard's hands as soon as possible.

But how?

The inn was full of armed friends. But their weapons were too dangerous to use. One false move, and Mery might lose her life.

His eyes lowered briefly to the poison ring that circled the spy's finger.

How had the villain managed to gain access to the prince's cup right under everyone's noses?

He'd used distraction. He'd loosened a brace beneath the platform, and while everyone's attention was focused on the collapsing stage, he'd slipped the poison into the cup.

Maybe Tristan could distract the spy.

He flipped the knife once in his hand and took a small step forward. The gesture wasn't threatening enough to goad the spy into action, just enough to get his attention.

Then he casually tossed the knife from hand to hand, not advancing, but not retreating either.

The spy frowned, clearly annoyed by his antics.

Tristan rolled the knife handle gracefully through his fingers and then twirled the blade atop his knuckles.

"Stop it," the spy growled.

With his right hand, Tristan whipped the knife straight up, making it tumble, end over end, in the air, and then caught it by the handle. Inching forward, he did it again. And again.

The last time he tossed it up, he intentionally missed the catch, sucking in a sharp breath as if the blade had sliced his fingers before it clattered to the floor at his feet.

But in that instant of inattention, Tristan used his left hand to knock the spy's knife hand aside. Then he gave the spy's wrist a hard chop to make him drop the stiletto.

The spy howled and squeezed his arm tighter around Mery's throat. She gagged, clawing at his forearm.

Tristan's heart seized. But he knew now it was a matter of brute force. The spy might be devious and clever. But Tristan had been working in the kitchens, hoisting cauldrons and heaving roasts, for most of his life. He could tear the villain limb from limb with his bare hands.

The coward must have seen the bloodlust in Tristan's eyes, for he released Mery all at once. When she pitched forward, Tristan caught her in his arms. The spy scrambled up the stairs and ducked into their bedchamber, slamming the door just before Rane's arrow struck it.

"The window!" Jossy yelled.

She and Rane turned and burst out the door of the inn to intercept the spy in case he tried to escape out the window. Drew and Lachlan stormed up the stairs to break down the bedchamber door.

But Tristan found his desire for revenge wasn't as powerful as his concern for Mery. The spy was cornered now. And he knew that without a hostage, the scrawny English bastard didn't stand a chance against a Viking huntsman, an old soldier, a woman warrior, and a champion golfer.

"Is it the bairn?" he asked, cradling Mery in his arms as they sat on the second stair.

"I think so." She squeezed his hand, and her brow creased in pain.

He flinched, feeling her pain almost as if it were his own. "'Twill be all right now," he said, as much to himself as to her. "Ye're safe."

Above them, the bedchamber door finally yielded to the pounding of Drew's longnose club and Lachlan's steel leg. Tristan heard shouting as the two warriors confronted the spy.

A moment later, Drew reemerged, shaking his head. "The coward's taken poison."

Tristan frowned. That wasn't good enough. Mery had taken poison, and she'd survived. "Make sure it works."

"Lachlan's got a blade on him," Drew said.

But then Mery let out a moan, and Tristan's attention was drawn immediately to her. His heart pounded as he realized the enormity of what was happening and how woefully inadequate he was to the task.

He could cook a banquet for three hundred guests. He could whip up a trifle at a moment's notice. He could butcher game from a morn's hunt and turn it into supper by nightfall. He could take scraps from a royal dinner and transform them into new dishes for servants.

But he didn't know the first thing about delivering a bairn.

Fortunately, Alisoune, Josselin, and Florie knew all about delivering bairns. Of course, it didn't make the process any quicker. As Mery labored in Jossy's bedchamber, she thought the stubborn creature would never come out of her.

But by breakfast the next morn, as she half-reclined on the bedchamber chair that Alisoune had cleverly modified into a birthing stool, the pains grew more fierce and closer together.

Mery began to bear down more forcefully, gripping Jossy's and Florie's hands. She could tell the bairn was about ready to make an appearance.

It seemed an equitable arrangement—a life for a death.

According to Jossy, the spy had died in the night. Rane had lugged the body far into the woods to bury in an unmarked grave. Meanwhile, Tristan had directed the kitchen staff to set the inn to rights. Jossy had reassured the guests that all the excitement was over and that nobody had ever had a petard. Lachlan was currently swapping war stories with some of the travelers by the fire. And Drew had taken the children out to teach Copernica how to golf.

"'Tis here," Mery groaned.

"Almost," Florie told her.

"Keep breathin', nice and deep," Jossy said.

"Ye know," Alisoune mused, "in China, new mothers eat the placenta after the—"

"Alisoune!" Florie and Jossy said together.

Alisoune nudged the spectacles up on her nose. "I just thought it was interestin'."

"Push!" Jossy barked.

Mery pushed, though she was getting a bit impatient with Jossy's commands.

"Is it crownin'?" Alisoune asked. "Let me see."

She squatted in front of Mery, examining her so closely that Mery wondered if she might dive inside.

"About an inch," she reported.

Mery couldn't push anymore. She let out her breath.

"Come on, Mery!" Jossy prodded.

"Don't tell me what to..." Mery's reprimand was swallowed up in another contraction. She pushed hard.

"That's it," Jossy said. "Keep it up."

After a long, fruitless push, Mery collapsed against the back of the chair, breathless. Why had she done this anyway? She didn't want to have this bairn. Not if it was going to be so much trouble.

"Nae," she murmured. "I'm done."

"Ye can do it," Florie said softly.

"'Twas about an inch and a half that time," Alisoune encouraged. "So if ye extrapolate at half an inch per contraction..."

"Fine, just leave it then," said Jossy, letting go of Mery's hand. "I didn't think ye could do it anyway."

The ladies' jaws dropped.

Jossy sniffed. "Ye're a bit frail, after all," she continued, "and ye don't have much stamina for a Highlander. I'm surprised ye made it this far."

While the other two stared at Jossy in silent shock, Mery felt her contraction and her ire building.

So impertinent Jossy didn't think she could do it? She'd show the sassy lass.

This time when the pressure gripped her, she surged forward with all her might.

A few moments later, a beautiful, slippery, miracle of a lass gushed out of her with a loud cry, announcing to Mery that she was a soprano.

After that, the women cheered and hugged, laughed and sobbed, forgave and forgot, whispered and cooed, kissed and coddled and comforted. And when Mery held the tiny, wet bairn in her arms, her eyes filled with tears.

Jossy apologized for goading her. Alisoune caught the afterbirth and tidied up. Florie made sure the bairn had all her fingers and toes and then swaddled her in linen.

Exhausted, Mery wanted to do nothing but hold her precious daughter and drift off to sleep.

But as she gazed at the lovely ladies who'd guided her through this latest adventure, she felt her heart swell with gratitude and affection. There was no one as sweet, spirited, bright, kindhearted, charming, magnificent, or powerful as a Scottish lass.

Now she had a Scottish lass of her own. She couldn't wait to show her to Tristan.

# epiLogue

"Maybe Meringue," Mery mused, gazing down at the lass in her arms as she sat beside Tristan on the bed.

His brows shot up. "Meringue MacKenzie?"

"I love meringues, And we could call her Meri for short, just like me."

His expression was so comical, she could hold back her laughter no longer.

He shook his head in self-mockery for ever believing her.

She gave their daughter a soft kiss on the brow and whispered, "Drew thinks we should call her Fairway."

"O' course he does. The man lives, breathes, and eats golf."

"And Alisoune didn't have enough children of her own to use up all the scientists' names, so she's given us a few options." Her lips twitched with amusement. "What do ye think o' Paracelsa or Leonarda?"

He shuddered.

The bairn squirmed in her sleep. Mery passed her to

Tristan, who cradled her as carefully as a sugar subtlety. She loved to see him holding their child.

"O' course," she said, "Rane thinks she should be named after a Vikin' goddess. And Jossy and Lachlan had a long list of warrior names. Florie suggested Amethyst, Emerald, or Garnet."

"Everyone has an opinion," he said with a sigh, tracing his daughter's brow with the tip of his finger.

"Oh, and Copernica insists we call her Progeny."

Tristan scowled. "I'm goin' to call her Greensleeves."

"Greensleeves?"

"'Tis my favorite song."

She smiled. That was the song she'd sung for him in the garden a year ago, right before they'd made wild, passionate love.

"Well, then Greensleeves 'tis. I'm glad that's decided."

She grinned at his nonsense. Greensleeves MacKenzie indeed. Her heart melted as she watched him fuss over their daughter as if she were the most precious dish he'd ever created. She knew he'd grapple with death to keep her safe.

There would be time to name her later. For now, it was enough that she was happy and healthy and had a set of lungs that would make her a fine soprano one day.

Like a Scottish thistle, she was lovely yet tough, beautiful yet prickly. And just like her mother, one day she'd find a strong and wise hero who could elude her thorns to discover the tender blossom within.

## The End

# Chank you for Reading my Book!

Did you enjoy it? If so, I hope you'll post a review to let others know! There's no greater gift you can give an author than spreading your love of her books.

It's truly a pleasure and a privilege to be able to share my stories with you. Knowing that my words have made you laugh, sigh, or touched a secret place in your heart is what keeps the wind beneath my wings. I hope you enjoyed our brief journey together, and may ALL of your adventures have happy endings!

If you'd like to keep in touch, feel free to sign up for my monthly e-newsletter at www.glynnis.net, and you'll be the first to find out about my new releases, special discounts, prizes, promotions, and more!

If you want to keep up with my daily escapades:
Friend me at facebook.com/GlynnisCampbell
Like my Page at bit.ly/GlynnisCampbellFBPage
Follow me at twitter.com/GlynnisCampbell
And if you're a super fan, join
facebook.com/GCReadersClan

# ɳATIVE GOLD

California Legends Book 1

Sakote had planned to snare a few squirrels today for the evening stew, but he'd left his hunting pouch at the waterfall. He frowned. He'd hoped to avoid places that would remind him of the white woman. But he had to retrieve it. The deerskin pouch was a gift from his father, and the tools in it—the snares, the knives, the mountain hemp line—would take days to replace.

So with a parcel of dried deer meat and a promise to his mother that he'd bring back some woodpecker feathers for her husband's *wahiete*—his ceremonial crown, Sakote set off for the waterfall.

The pouch was where he'd left it, beside the great boulder. But he couldn't help searching the wet banks of the pool, looking for some sign of the woman who'd come here with him. There was nothing. She'd left behind no scrap of cloth, no scent, not even a footprint.

Of course, that didn't mean her spirit was gone. She lingered here still—in the gurgle of water over the stones, so much like her laughter, in the verdant depths of the pool, like her eyes, and in the heat of the sun upon his shoulder, reminding him of the warmth of her arms around him.

"Damn!" There were no words of anger or frustration in Sakote's language, so he borrowed the curse from the white man.

It didn't matter what the elders said, what the dream tried to tell him, how tempting Mati was. He must follow the old ways, the ways of the Konkow, or they would be lost. The white woman showed him another path, a dangerous path, a path he must not take.

The sun continued to blaze upon his back, and he knew a quick swim in the pond would cool his blood. He took off his moccasins, freed his hair, and loosened the thong around his breechcloth, letting it fall to the ground. Climbing to the crest of the boulder, he took a full breath and dove into the shimmering midst of the pool.

The bracing water sizzled over his skin as he plunged deep through the waves. The chill current swept past his body, swirling his hair like the long underwater moss, washing away his thoughts.

He broke the surface and shook his hair back, then swam for the waterfall. It pounded the rock like a *kilemi*, a log drum, and made a mist that hid the small cave behind the fall. He climbed out onto the slippery ledge and stood up, easing forward into the path of the fall, where it pummeled him with punishing force, driving white spears into his bent back and shoulders. The pounding awakened his body and challenged him. He slowly raised his head, braced his feet, reached toward the sky with outstretched arms, and withstood the heavy fall of water with a triumphant smile.

Unfortunately, the loud thunder of the fall prevented him from hearing that he was no longer alone at the pool.

Mattie's jaw dropped. Her breath caught.

After sketching miners all morning, she'd decided to make a few drawings of the waterfall. She remembered the way there, and though she might have hoped the Indian would return, she didn't really expect him. The fact that he had indeed come back, and in such bold display, couldn't have amazed her more.

What in God's name was he doing? He stood at the foot of the waterfall, as bare as the day he was born, letting the water beat him within an inch of his life and grinning all the while.

She thought to yell out to him, to reprimand him for such indecent behavior, such outrageous liberties, such flagrant...but then the artist came out in her. She realized that what she beheld was beautiful, that *he* was beautiful. Watching him in all his naked glory was like witnessing the birth of a god.

She perched on a rock wedged between two trees, hoping the lush foliage and her drab plaid dress would conceal her. She found an empty page and set to work sketching.

He couldn't remain there long, she knew, or else he'd be pounded into the rock. She had to work quickly, penciling in the bare bones and trusting the rest to memory.

Sure enough, just as she finished the roughest of renderings, he brought his arms down through the fall like great white wings and dove into the middle of the pool.

His naked body slicing through the water sent a rush of delicious fire through her. Her pencil hovered over the page. It was wrong, what she did, spying on him and sketching him in his altogether without his knowledge. And yet, she thought, patting a cheek grown hot with impropriety, it felt so right.

He bobbed up and flung his hair back, spraying droplets of water across the rippling surface.

Mattie pressed her pencil against her lower lip.

He swam forward, gliding through the waves as smoothly as a trout. Then he wheeled over onto his back and floated on the surface, boldly facing the midday sun like some pagan sacrifice.

Mattie's teeth sank into the pencil.

She could see everything—the naked sprawl of his limbs, the corona of his long ebony hair, the dark patch at the juncture of his thighs, and its manly treasure, set like a jewel on black velvet.

He was Adam. Or Adonis. He was Icarus fallen from the sky. Hera cast into the sea. As innocent as an angel. As darkly beautiful as Lucifer.

Mattie blushed to the tips of her toes. She most definitely should not be witness to this...this...she had no word for his wanton display, but she was sure it was completely indecent. Still she couldn't tear her eyes away. He was utterly, irrefutably perfect. And looking at him left her faint with a mixture of emotions as dizzying as whiskey and as unstable as gunpowder.

She slid the pencil from between her lips, flipped to a new page, and began to draw. Despite her rattled nerves, her hand was steady, for she captured every nuance of shade, every subtle contour, each flash of translucence, as if the water lived and moved upon the paper. And the man... He was so true to life that she half expected the figure to lazily pitch over and swim off the page.

A fern tickled her nose, and she brushed it back, and then leaned forward to put the finishing touches on the portrait—a few more branches dabbling in the waves, a leaf floating by his head. She decided on the title, scribbling it at the bottom beside her signature.

Just in time. The Indian knifed under, a flash of sculpted buttocks and long legs, disappearing beneath the surface and into the emerald depths.

Sakote saw the movement of branches from the corner of his eye, but gave no indication. If it was a deer, he didn't want to frighten it from its drinking place. If it was a bear, his splashing would scare it soon enough. If it was a *willa*, he'd have to be clever. He floated a moment more, letting the waves carry him gently toward the deepest part of the pool, watching for sudden movements through the dark lashes of his eyes. Then he gulped in a great breath and dove to the bottom, where the water was cold and shadowy.

He came up silently on the concealed side of the big granite boulder and eased his way out of the water and around the rock until he could see what hid in the brush.

Mati.

She wore another ugly brown dress with lines of other colors running through it like mistakes, and her hair was captured into a tight knot at the back of her head. She bit at her lower lip and leaned out dangerously far between two dogwood saplings, shielding her eyes with one hand, searching the pool for him.

Sakote didn't know what he felt. Joy. Or anger. Relief. Dread. Or desire.

Worry wrinkled her brow, and she leaned forward even farther, bending the saplings almost to the breaking point.

"Oh, no," she murmured.

Her words were only a breath of a whisper on the

breeze, but they carried to his ears like sad music. Mati edged between the two trees and took three slippery steps down the slope. Meanwhile, Sakote moved in the opposite direction, up the rise. While she scanned the water, he crept behind her, stopping when he found the sketchbook on the ground, frowning when he saw the figure floating on the page.

Now he knew what he felt. Fury. He glanced down at his naked body, at his man's pride, shrunken with cold to the size of an acorn, then at its perfect duplicate drawn on the paper. And he felt as if he would explode with rage.

He must have made a sound, some strangled snarl of anger, for Mati turned. And screamed.

# ABOUT THE AUTHOR

I'm a *USA Today* bestselling author of swashbuckling action-adventure historical romances, mostly set in Scotland, with over a dozen award-winning books published in six languages.

But before my role as a medieval matchmaker, I sang in *The Pinups,* an all-girl band on CBS Records, and provided voices for the MTV animated series *The Maxx,* Blizzard's *Diablo* and *Starcraft* video games, and *Star Wars* audiobooks.

I'm the wife of a rock star (if you want to know which one, contact me) and the mother of two young adults. I do my best writing on cruise ships, in Scottish castles, on my husband's tour bus, and at home in my sunny southern California garden.

I love transporting readers to a place where the bold heroes have endearing flaws, the women are stronger than they look, the land is lush and untamed, and chivalry is alive and well!

I'm always delighted to hear from my readers, so please feel free to email me at glynnis@glynnis.net. And if you're a super-fan who would like to join my inner circle, sign up at http://www.facebook.com/GCReadersClan, where you'll get glimpses behind the scenes, sneak peeks of works-in-progress, and extra special surprises.